GM & GS PRIVATE INVESTIGATION SERVICE

BOOK II

D. H. CROSBY

authorHOUSE®

AuthorHouse™
1663 Liberty Drive
Bloomington, IN 47403
www.authorhouse.com
Phone: 1 (800) 839-8640

Published by AuthorHouse 12/15/2016

ISBN: 978-1-5246-5502-0 (sc)
ISBN: 978-1-5246-5501-3 (e)

Library of Congress Control Number: 2016919252

Print information available on the last page.

PART FIVE

CHAPTER ONE

When Adam finally got home from his construction job, he was exhausted. He put his nasty little lunchbox on the shaky table. In comes his brother named Tate, who plopped down in the chair beside him.

He spoke with a lisp, "Did you talk to Chris today?"

"Aye, what's it to you?" Adam was in no mood for his little brother's nonsense.

"I just wanted to know he is. He always liked me to call him Daddy. Isn't that a hoot?"

"He ain't fit to be a daddy. Your daddy or no one else's daddy. All he knows … is the war … and the enemy has got to be attacked with grenades and pipe bombs. You crazy kid stay away from those friends of Chris."

"They will get your ass in trouble!" He was standing over Tate now and staring down at him.

"I mean it not another word about Chris! Do you hear me?" Tate was moving his chair up against the wall.

"Yes sir, you sound just like a drill sergeant and I can't wait to join the Army and get away from you."

He was barely sixteen and Adam had raised him since their mom had died. He had never knew who his Dad was.

He had done the best he could do for the boy, but those so-called friends were cheap little punks. He grimaced and shook his head.

If he didn't have to fulfill his obligation to Chris, he'd take the boy in a different direction than the one he was headed in.

"What's the use in talking to you … you're gonna to do what you want to do anyways. I wish someone had talked some sense into me at your age, but I'm too far gone. Did you eat yet?" Adam asked as he walked back around the table.

"Yea, Yea, with the punks! We grabbed a hamburger."

"Where'd you get the money?" walking toward the door.

"I stole a pack of cigarettes from the store up the street and bought a hamburger. No big deal!" Tate quickly raised his arms up covering his face. Adam was red-faced and when that happened he was about to blow.

"That's it! You are going to your Aunt Eunice's," Adam walked to block the door.

"Until you learn some sense. She will beat the tar out of you, if you don't behave … I can't do it … OR I'd end up under the jail."

"Which I probably will anyways," thinking to himself.

Tate was in shock. Adam had never said that to him before and he knew he meant it.

"Get your clothes together … And don't you dare think about going outta that window or you will be sorry!" Adam said and he broadened his stance at Tate's bedroom door. If he tried Adam would surely tackle him.

"I called her earlier today so don't think she doesn't know we are coming. Now hop to it!"

Tate was gathering his few worldly belongings and shoving them into a large paper bag. He was done but he had a question for Adam.

"What did you mean by you were headed under the jail?" Tate mumbled.

"Ain't nothing kid … just a figure of speech," patting him on the back. That kid missed nothing. They walked to the old rundown truck, without a word being spoken.

The next Adam purchased a few things at Walmart and a few things at the hardware store. He had his homemade bomb materials just like cousin Chris had taught him. The device had to be placed just right in the elevator.

He had to be in sight of the elevator to trigger it with his cell phone. He must see the main person Chris wanted him to waste … Guy would be in that elevator when the time came.

Now it was just a matter of biding his time. Doing his construction job as usual.

He was thinking Chris had always sent him money for Tate through the years. Aunt Eunice finally told him … that … Chris was Tate and HIS real father. So this favor he was doing for his cousin, was really for his father.

Roscoe's honeymoon was over and he went to the Security Building. He strolled in and there they were. All eyes on him.

They were up to something, he could smell it in the air.

His nose went straight to the coffeepot. He stood erect and sipped his coffee. Taking in all the teasing that they were throwing at him, and making a mental note of whom, he had to payback in the future.

"This team of mine, Damn they are a pain."

Inscoe said, "I saw you walking wide legged through the door, Boss. So I went and got you an ice pack for your balls!"

They all roared and said in unison, "Welcome back, Roscoe. We have all missed you!" they lowered a banner with all their names on it and 2 wedding bells.

Then his secretary brought a cake out with handcuffs on it. There was a bride figurine in the center of one handcuff and a groom figure in the center of the other handcuff.

He shut his eyes, he always did when he thought he was going to tear up.

He said in an authoritative voice, "You guys are the best! Mere words cannot express how I intend to pay you back.

Enough said," and he singled Inscoe out with a nod.

"You ladies know my Beatrice well and she definitely has me handcuffed to her forever. That was spot on!" bowing to them.

"Now let's eat cake while the coffee is hot … because it will not be anymore goofing off from this day forward. We have some serious business to discuss and the details are still coming in" He walked to the cake and asked,

"How do you cut this thing?"

"With a knife, darling!"

He turned and there she stood with a long knife in her hand. Twirling it like a baton and she walked to the cake and cut it like she was serving a teapot soiree.

She looked so prim and proper in a new outfit from Paris that her mother had given to her for a wedding present. She was walking that walk toward him and he sat down at the table.

"They invited me!" and whispered to him. "I am glad you sat down otherwise we both would have been embarrassed."

She cut her a piece of cake and sat down beside him.

"Oh Hell!" he said to himself. "She had better not take that shoe off and rub his shin."

To her he said politely, "Be a good wife and pour me a cup of coffee and for heaven sakes keep your shoes on."

"Of course! But first I have to get my handcuffs off the cake ... I have plans for them."

He saw her dropping them in her purse and then she walked very slowly back to the table.

While she was gone, he flagged Inscoe down and asked pitifully, "Can you get me another ice pack. Be discreet."

"Thank God for emergency supplies," he said to himself.

Turning to Inscoe, "Thank you old buddy!"

"Anytime Boss, just give me a holler," and he walked to the other side of the room.

Now Beatrice could talk all she wants. He stretched his neck like he had this one under control.

She did take off her shoe as she was eating her cake and slowly turning to him. Whispered in his ear, "Do you need me to get some more ice for you, Dear?" smiling as she rubbed her toe up and down his shin.

"A two ton truckload would be nice right about now, Darling!"

"I saw what you did with those handcuffs, Dear!"

"Those are my personal set and I plan to get them back," and he acted like he was going to get up.

"OK, I will behave. Just keep seated. I don't want any of these hussies panting after my husband after I go home. Why don't we go into your office?" "No way! Go home!" He was almost shouting. "I have a business meeting in ten minutes."

Everyone was mumbling and one lady said, "I guess the honeymoon is over!" and her group giggled.

The other woman said, "Mine only last two days!"

She continued, "He died in bed!"

Another woman said, "I am so sorry!"

The woman said, "Don't be. He died happy and I got his insurance policy. It was a win-win situation!"

They laughed and she said afterward, "I was just kidding you'all, but I have dreamt that! If I had gotten a big insurance check, do you think I would be working here?" then they were all laughing loudly.

Some of the male security guards shouted, "Can you ladies over there be a little quieter. You are disturbing the peace!"

Roscoe knew he had to stand and get them back to work.

"Beatrice you promised ... now sit on your hands," he whispered as he rose.

"Hey guys, thanks again but we have got to get back to work! WE got a meeting in the conference room in ten minutes."

Roscoe walked Beatrice to her car quickly. It was a cute little red Miata convertible and how she got those beautiful long legs in that car, he would never know.

He would focus on the meeting and kiss her on the cheek swiftly.

"That is the kiss I will remember … when I cuff you to the bed tonight and have my way with you!" then she was gone.

He was standing there looking into the sky when Inscoe blew his whistle, "Come on in Boss! We got a meeting!"

"Inscoe what is my name?" At this moment I can't remember, all I can remember is what my wife said. She has that effect on me....! Roscoe turned and walked with Inscoe toward the building.

"Boss what in the world has you so rattled?"

"She … he began to stutter, "told me what she intended to do to me with those handcuffs … that is all I can say!"

"This phase will pass and in a year will sitting as far away from each other as you can get. Trust me. I have been through it and lived to tell about it."

"OK! But she wants a baby and wants it now. Four or five times a day is killing me!" then a smile came over his face.

Inscoe about swallowed his tongue and his eyes were bulging, "You are kidding. Aren't you?"

"Nope a year from now … we may have twins or triplets sitting between us. She has a family history of that!"

"Boss... pull yourself together … we got a meeting! Walk fast, they are waiting!"

Roscoe conducted the meeting with ease. Filling in all of the details of Lefty, Frank and Adam at the construction site.

He reviewed on a wall map the property at the lake. His house on one slide . Guy's house on another slide. He restated what security he wanted at the job site. He wanted to insure that the coverage of his family was still 24/7. He knew that Beatrice had a guard that was following her everywhere she went, now that he was back to work.

CHAPTER TWO

He sat down at his desk and Trevor called. He asked if he was in his secure office. He was told to lock his door, so no one could come in or listen in their conversation.

He briefed him on Jeff and Lance.

Roscoe asked, "Why would we need two sharpshooters?"

Trevor had to think quickly, if Roscoe knew he suspected that Jeff of flubbing his mission and getting Beatrice shot, he would be after him and kill him with his own bare hands.

"We just need one in Dallas and one in Hendersonville. You have to know what Guy discovered. Yes, in Kyleigh's phone camera background was Bruce's face. That was spine tinkling. So I have my SBI and FBI buddies snooping around. We are assured by the prison system warden that Bruce has not escaped."

"What do you think is happening? Someone is definitely too close to Kyleigh. Guy is probably going crazy," Roscoe was trying to absorb all this information at once.

"I think it is another person as before with a mask of Bruce's face. I know you are probably going to have some flashbacks, son." Taking a deep breath Trevor continued, "but I had to tell you. I will leave it up to you, if you want to tell Beatrice," Trevor paused.

"The last thing I have to tell you is Bruce wrote a letter to Guy a week before Kyleigh was told by her doctor that she was pregnant. Get this … he told Guy to take care of his grandson. We think there is a mole, either in the facility where she was, or in the lab testing department which is separate from the facility. The doctor told Guy he didn't want to tell her earlier because he didn't want to upset her mental state. He had known for a month. She has been so excited and wants to come home when their house is finished. She is here at the ranch for the time being. That is a SECRET because Kyleigh wants to tell Beatrice first," Trevor paused again.

He knew this was a lot of detailed information for Roscoe to process at once, but he had to put all the cards on the table.

"Back to this information that Bruce got in prison about the pregnancy could have been very profitable for someone. He has many contacts on the outside. We must find out … if these masks are controlled by him. Since he by telephone gave the word to have Beatrice killed. That is the question, whether this man or men are controlled by Bruce. Roscoe are you there?"

"Yes I am trying to make sense out of all of this. The same masks that were worn to hurt my Beatrice … they could be here as well as there … depending on where Guy and Kyleigh are living. Is this right?"

"Yes….." that was all Trevor could say.

"My BeBe wants to have kids right away. She asked and I said okay." He had to tell Trevor. "Wouldn't it be a hoot? If in a year, you and grandma had a house full of grandchildren running around!" Roscoe was ventilating to another man that he does want to have kids.

"You know I was adopted ...and it put a bad taste in my mouth about having children. But now all I want is a little red haired green eyed boy or girl. Is there anything else I need to know?" Roscoe was like a zombie. Pale and walking on cruise control as he walked around the office and talked into the phone.

"No... son. That's it. Remember don't tell Beatrice about the baby or Madeline will have my head. She said Kyleigh wants to tell her herself. Bye for now. Love you two!"

Trevor hung the phone up and unlocked his office door.

Madeline and Kyleigh were hoeing in the garden spot.

Kyleigh said, "This is like old times in Hendersonville. Didn't we have the most beautiful garden? You and I," she was beaming and her smile was as bright as the morning sun.

"Yes. It was the best! I have missed that as much as you have," Madeline agreed and smiled at her dear Kyleigh.

All of a sudden a slew of dogs came bounding around the corner of the house.

"Trevor must be home and let the dogs out," at that moment her dog Blackie jumped on her chest and got a good petting from her master.

Black Velvet bounded straight into Kyleigh's lap, and began licking her master's face as if she belonged there.

Trevor came around the corner, "I see you two girls are being well loved! I'm jealous! Just joking... I love to see my girls happy."

When Guy got home, they had a good old barbeque at the pit. The guards were invited. They coordinated their watch and it gave Trevor and Guy a chance to quiz them. Even when you do background checks, the one to one interaction with someone always is the best indicator of a man's true character.

Trevor said, "Seems like we have a good bunch of men, Guy. So relax!" sipping his martini. Madeline had fixed it for him, but he preferred brandy. Anything his little woman wanted him to try, he would gladly. Raising his glass and smiling, he nodded to her as if he liked it.

"Can't relax! Haven't done that in a long time!" raising his glass to smile at Kyleigh. "Whoever heard of grown men drinking martinis at a BBQ? I'd rather have a beer."

They both laughed so hard they were coming to join in on their amusement.

Kyleigh had on a cute flowery beach ensemble and Madeline was dressed to the nines in her Coco Chanel. She turned to Kyleigh and said, "Whomever heard of wearing our outfits to a BBQ, but whatever that hunk of a man wants me to where, I will. I'd rather have shorts on. How about you?" then both the women began to laugh.

Kyleigh said, "I don't have any choice I can't button my jeans anymore," and grinned at grandma.

Madeline said, "We must go shopping for some proper maternity clothes. Did you want to go into the city or shop online with me?"

"I would like to stay as far away from the big city as I can, you understand me better than anyone. Always have," tears were forming in Kyleigh's eyes.

"OK, dear! Let's tell the guys. WE are going shopping!"

Madeline added, "Trevor just loves for me to shop, but I love my jeans and cowboy boots."

Grinning at Trevor as she and Kyleigh approached the men.

"Watch out Guy! They are plotting something, I can see it in your grandma's eyes!" and chugged down the martini and walked to met them.

Guy did the same and added, "Yeah we are so hen-pecked!" looking at Trevor and laughing.

This night had been just what they all had needed.

"Kyleigh are you going into town?" Guy asked.

"No dear, your grandma has convinced me to shop online," winking at him.

GS blew Madeline a kiss and mouthed, "Thank you!"

GM came over and kissed her hand and slapped it on the back of his neck.

"You are welcome, grandson. We are back to normal."

Beatrice was having lunch with her highbrow of a mother at the town's THE INN. It served first-class quality cuisine and was a place that her mother brought her when she was little.

"You look beautiful today, Momma. Is that a new creation you have on?" her mother loved to be complimented on about her tailored clothing.

"Why yes, my BeBe. You always notice, my love."

Inga was a superb seamstress who came many years ago to America from Hungary to pursue her dream of designing. She had met her husband Roberto, a New Yorker, and fell madly in love.

They had BeBe their first year of marriage. Her dreams were put on hold. They had advanced their skills in tailoring in this little town, and sent some designs in to the prominent House of Design.

They were asked to come and apply for a position. They were told there was a need for new artists, so they did. They moved when BeBe was a teenager. Her daughter was not happy in the big city and missed her friends.

She was a good girl and she did everything they wanted her to do. They had wanted BeBe to design and she tried. They wanted her to model and she tried, but they could see she had an eye for architecture.

She dearly loved it. They had sent her to school for this and she had excelled. They sat in THE INN reminiscing about the past. They mentioned nothing... no not one word about the kidnapping... not one word about the kidnapping. They had agreed awhile back to leave it in the past, her mother had said.

"What's my BeBe been up to?" Inga asked sipping her Minestrone soup.

"Making a baby, Momma!" Beatrice knew that would make her pristine mother squeal.

"Now ... BeBe don't talk like that in public. In private, I will celebrate," breaking her crescent roll to stifle the rest of what she wanted to say.

"Don't be embarrassed Momma. We are back at home where people speak how they feel," she paused to sip her iced tea.

"Then she said, "No one looks down on you here for being yourself," smiling at her mother.

Grateful her mother and father were alive, Beatrice wanted them to be happy and not afraid.

Her mother nodded, "And how is that wonderful son-in-law of mine doing?" Her mother thought the sun rose and set because of Roscoe. He had saved them because of his police work and his contacts.

"He is a happy man and he sends his love. He has been awful busy with our house and Guy's house. Soon we will have you over. Tell poppa we love him too," while scooping her strawberry shortcake up as gracefully as she could.

"Busy on his honeymoon. Not on his house," and she covered her mouth so she could giggle into it.

Inga thought of how wonderful Roscoe had been to her BeBe while she was in the hospital.

"Your father was like Roscoe that first year … very busy," she laughed. "You said I could say what I thought," and they both giggled.

"This is our town and we will never live anywhere else, my BeBe. I have never told you how sorry we are that we dragged you to New York. Can you ever forgive this old woman?" Inga pleaded.

Beatrice reached across and cupped her mother's face, "Never worry about that ever. Ever … it was a learning experience. It is why I love this town and I love you. All we have to do is make new memories," Beatrice sighed.

"She had to change the subject before her mother would cry,

"Do you want to take poppa anything?"

"No dear," she grinned.

"He is a busy man ... busy fixing me a gourmet supper. Busy busy, that man is!"

They both giggled. She had learned so many things from her mother but most of all to make her man happy. She had always said, "There will be good times, Bebe and there will be bad times. Enjoy each … because if you didn't have bad times, honey … you would not know how to appreciate the good times," and she would smile and pat her on the cheek.

They kissed and off they went, to meet the men in their lives to make their day, a happy one.

CHAPTER THREE

It had been three weeks and the house for Guy and Kyleigh was almost finished. The multiple crews were still working around the clock.

The back driveway and elevator had been installed this week without a problem. The landscapers had been feverishly working on the design of the shrubberies and the magnolia trees because they were Kyleigh's favorite.

Plants of lavender were to be in the foreground with fuchsia of pink and white throughout the flowerbeds in the front and in the back. This was the only request that Kyleigh had, and she said Beatrice knew exactly how she wanted everything else.

The plane had set down and Guy and Kyleigh were met by Roscoe and Beatrice. Of course, there were many extra guards with them this time. Guy had told Roscoe to make sure so Kyleigh would feel safe.

Kyleigh ran to Beatrice and hugged her. While Guy was shouting, "Woman don't you dare run. I say don't you. Please don't run sweetheart!"

He caught up with her as she was hugging Beatrice.

"He's such a fuddy -duddy. Pay him no mind. Ever since

he found out that I was pregnant, he has smothered me. Won't let me do a darn thing," Kyleigh stood pouting. Then she added, "but I love it! How do you like my first maternity smock Beatrice?" twirling in front of a frowning Guy.

"Beatrice you will house us … until our house is truly finished?'

"You look beautiful in anything … you little pixie! You can wear anything and it looks good. Even a burlap sack would. I have missed you so," hugging her and putting her arm around her shoulder.

"Where else would you stay. Madeline is still in Dallas and the boys have a lot to catch up on … as we do. Makes sense to me!" Beatrice spouted so the 'boys' could hear.

"I, second the motion sweet wife of mine. They definitely will stay with us, not at grandma's," Roscoe said in his most authoritative voice.

"Has he been bossing you around Beatrice?"

"You betcha and I love it!" and they giggled.

Nothing prepared Guy and Kyleigh for the view at the lake with the two huge mansions on either side of it and the mountains on the horizon. They hugged each other.

This was where he taught he the meaning of more ...more... more … and if Guy's done his math right where their baby had been conceived.

"We are home, sweetheart," kissing Kyleigh as if no one was around.

Roscoe kissed Kyleigh on the cheek. "I'll not show off on the first day that they are back. Let them have their glory, but tonight you are mine," looking at her as if he could devour her in one bite.

"I understand ... my dear husband," Beatrice winked.

She leaned over and whispered in his ear, "If ever we get started it would take more than a few guards to pull us apart," she watched his Adam's apple go up and down as he gulped…he closed his eyes.

"You know I creamed in my jeans at that thought," he admitted. "Damn, you are the best! Maybe we should let them go on by themselves and we visit the Silverado?"

She twirled like Kyleigh and got a far distance away from him and grabbed Kyleigh's hand.

They walked and talked all the way from the long white limo that had brought them home.

"Kyleigh you have saved me, he was going to ravish me," Beatrice said and they started giggling.

"They are definitely brothers. Aren't they cute?" Kyleigh said.

"Yeah they are … but mine looks like he has spilled his drink in his lap," Beatrice said.

"Yeah I believe you are right. Won't be long before you will be pregnant by the looks of things," raising her eyebrows.

"Stop that K. Look at your own man," Beatrice said with a pretend pouty lip.

"You are right! I will devour my own man tonight! Pregnancy only HEIGHTENS your sex drive, BeBe!"

"Please don't tell me that K. If I was more heightened you would have to scrape me off of the ceiling. Roscoe and I are about to kill ourselves as it is … OMG I think I just creamed in my panties just thinking about it," and they both hollered.

"Not only can men talk trash, we women can too!"

"Just like middle school K … we would tell each other everything!"

"Everything BeBe ... every single detail!" said Kyleigh.

They screamed with laughter.

The men came running to see what was the matter.

There they stood staring deep into each of their own husbands' eyes.

Guy told Roscoe, "Looks like we are in a heap of trouble. Are there two bedrooms far far apart?"

Roscoe looking into Beatrice's eyes, "I can call you a cab, Bro. This limo is mine … Just" gulping. "Say the word? And yes … our master bedroom and the other two bedrooms are way way away from each other!"

"When do we get a break?" Guy asked.

"I don't want a break. My wife wants a baby! So four times a day I service her to make sure her wish comes true. This service is in my pants, Bro."

"This white limo was our honeymoon suite and just looking at it has me all fired up. Damn, now I am all wet!" Guy looked at Roscoe, "Just like junior high! We told each other everything … every frigging time we ….!"

"Yep ... every time we shared our missed firings!"

They both howled.

The girls were at the limo by then.

Kyleigh looked at Beatrice and said, "I wonder what that was all about?"

"I've no clue BUT it looks like your man has spilled his drink in his lap, too!" they both shook their heads.

The guards said to each other, "These people are nuts!"

On the drive home Beatrice had sat with Kyleigh on one side, and Roscoe and Guy on the other, but now they are going to get their own space.

Beatrice said, "We better hurry and choose your bedroom before one of them hurts themselves."

"You are right. It will take them awhile to get our luggage in the house. We must show them where to put it!" Kyleigh added, "I love your house! Just like we drew it in middle school. I will see it later!" rounding the long hall to an enormous bedroom.

"If this is the one you like I will phone Roscoe. The only thing wrong with this house is ... it is soooo big! Even for us giraffes!"

They both sat down on the large sofa that matched the bedding and drapes while Beatrice called Roscoe.

She said, "Roscoe we are in the east wing bedroom and Kyleigh is tired and I think she wants to take a nap. Will you hurry honey with the … luggage!"

"That I will … bring them in a hurry, sweetie!"

"Just the mention of … luggage and Roscoe starts to drool...about his daily luggage. That's our cue and he brings it to me!"

They were laughing hysterically when Guy and Roscoe opened the bedroom door.

"Just want to show you the intercom on each wall and make sure it is OFF," she paused. "When you are bathing etc etc..." Beatrice blushed. Kyleigh didn't.

"Thanks for that info... I think I will lie down for a little bit.

Guy can you, darling ...put that itsy-bitsy makeup bag and toiletries in the bathroom … all else I can put away later."

Kyleigh did a swan dive for the bed.

"That's our cue to leave and … if you two need anything

just holler. We will see you at dinner around 8:00PM. Roscoe left the bedroom pulling Beatrice right behind him.

She had her hand on his butt walking to their bedroom.

Teasing he said, "Are you going to take a nap at this time of day?"

BeBe shook her head, "You betcha!" and her index was waving for him to follow her. "Come to mama!"

Roscoe slowly entered the office building to make his rounds and make sure everyone was watching the construction site and his home. Nothing was new, so he went into his office, locked the door, and caught a hour power nap.

He knew he surely could not get a nap at home. Stretching he got up and looked out the window and there was a man with a Bruce MASK, peering from the adjoining building right into his office.

He announced it on the intercom to all officers in detail. He described the man and said, "Get that man!... and get him now! By all accounts this is the enemy. They have arrrived!"

He had to alert Guy "I hate to call, but you have to know this without the girls knowing. The mask men have arrived. There is one on the building across from me. My men are after him. You and the girls stay put," and he hung up.

CHAPTER FOUR

The man was captured. He was Japanese. After much interrogation, he admitted he worked for Bruce. He would not give any information about any men that might have been with him.

At least, they had a mask that was intact and a suspect linked to the airport shooting. He notified the police and SBI and they notified the FBI.

They had enough man power to find anyone else that maybe out there.

When the undercover FBI agent was browsing around the parking area at Guy's new house. He noticed the workers were in groups, but this one guy was not. He decided to follow him and notified three other agents to surround the area. Frank was notified that the FBI was on the grounds.

He in turn found Lefty, "You steer clear. I know you want him, if it is Adam, but let the professionals do their job. You and I can take a supper break. What do you say?"

"This is personal! But I don't want to get in the way! And if I saw him I would definitely be in the way! Thank you!" and Lefty patted Frank on the back this time.

A few construction workers saw that and one said to the other, "Frank is going to slug that fool any minute. No one puts their hands on the boss!"

Instead they saw them sit down and ate their supper that they had brought in lunchboxes.

The agent followed Adam with his lunchbox that was larger than most. He sat it down by the elevator and took several articles out of his coat pocket.

"Don't let that creep get on that elevator!" he spoke into his shoulder mike to the other agents. At this area of the house, they knew it had past inspection several days ago. It was posted, "OFF LIMITS TO ALL PERSONNEL."

They zeroed in on him at the elevator and apprehended Adam without a hassle. He was read his rights, handcuffed and taken away after being thoroughly searched.

In the lunchbox were all the materials to make a bomb on the spot. The materials were labeled for evidence. Separate the materials were of no danger. If he had gotten into the elevator and placed it with the timer he had, it would have destroyed one half of the house if not all of it.

The agents notified Roscoe and he fell onto his knees in front of all of his staff, "Thank you God" and rose and explained his gratitude.

The day before he had himself rode on that elevator with the superintendent. He would not have suspected this to be the place his brother or family member would have been murdered.

If he had not called in the FBI for the mask man, someone would have died.

The mask man said he was there to protect the Smiths not to harm them, and no one believed him. Could Bruce,

Guy's father have sent him to help Guy? Were there others? The police would have to find that out.

They would let Roscoe know.

This though would be all over the TV. The capture of a attempted bomber at Guy's house.

He had to prepare Guy. He wanted him to prepare Kyleigh. He would speak to Beatrice. So if Kyleigh has a relapse they will have the family doctor called.

He was able to get through to him on the first ring.

"Keep all TVs in the house off and no radios on either!"

He had called Beatrice first so she was on the phone with the doctor. He said he would be glad to come, if needed.

All avenues were covered and the construction continued. The FBI had closed the entrance to the construction site. Two officers were posted to check all ID badges before admittance.

The TV crews were kept at a distance on the opposite side of the house and not in eye view of Roscoe's house, but the helicopters were swarming.

He had to call Trevor and Madeline.

Jeff had come to Roscoe's office as soon as he heard the TV report. Roscoe told him he still may be needed encase there were other masked men with Bruce's face on them.

Jeff's face went white. "I just had a flashback and I know your wife has them, too. I still wake up at night and think about how I missed, and almost cost her life."

"The second shot saved her. We will always be forever grateful," shaking Jeff's hand.

How could he tell Roscoe that he had not shot twice, but he was the one that ordered her killed. All he wanted was the COCAINE. He had got hooked on it in Vietnam ... and his habit was enormous. He was sweating as they spoke.

"NO need for thanks. Trevor coming in?" Jeff asked.

"Yea he should be on his way!" Roscoe said.

"See ya!" Jeff was out the door. His nose was runny and the withdrawals from the heroin he had took, in place of the cocaine, was kicking his ass.

If he had just got that load in the safety deposit box at the airport that day, he wouldn't be in the fix he was in now.

He was getting a steady shipment from Jared Banks and now the bastard was dead. The ninjas that Bruce had sent, will never stop me. I killed that one at the airport because he was shooting at me, not Beatrice .... my bullet is what hit her.

He went straight to the airport and booked a flight out.

Vietnam was his destination, never would he come back to the states.

Lance Lonestar had followed him and saw Jeff buy the heroin and how bad he was shaking today. He just saw him get on an airplane bound for Vietnam. He checked ... it was a one way flight. Lance would tell Trevor, his true friend of what he had learned.

Trevor was coming in from Dallas to the Charlotte Airport.

Their luggage was being loaded into the white limo by James.

Then he looked up and saw his buddy, Lance.

He told Madeline that he had to speak to a friend and that he would be right back. Lance filled him in and he was visibly angry.

"What a piece of sh--!" he began pacing and Lance walked with him.

"I know Trev ... but you had no way of knowing. A lot of us have ... had life throw us a curve!"

"I trusted the wrong man!" wiping the sweat from his forehead. His anger made him break out in a cold sweat. Just like when they were in the force. Flashbacks of what a good friend Jeff had been.

"This to will come to past. Don't beat yourself up. Promise me you will call if you ever need me again... Semper fi!" He gave Trevor a bear hug before walking off.

"Trevor told Madeline what had happened with Jeff and finally all the details he had kept her pretty little head from worrying about. She was angry and that was natural.

Then she punched him with her fist, "Don't you ever do that again. You … You … We are married now. We are a team. I can handle most anything and have for many years!"

"I know dear but I will protect you till the last breath I take.

Watch the road James," and he closed the privacy window and kissed Madeline like she had never been kissed.

"Now say it, Madeline. That you forgive me!"

"You are forgiven."

Sixty minutes later, they were driving up Roscoe's driveway. Roscoe had kept all the TVs and radios off. Because they didn't know how Kyleigh would react when she hears.

"We will talk to the boys in private until we find out, what they have told her," and he took her hand and escorted her to the door of this grand mansion.

"I agree that is wise. I will talk to the boys … I mean men.

I will talk to the men, Madeline. We must face it. We are getting old!" Trevor said.

"Not me. You maybe. I'm going to get Botox every

chance I get and stay forever young … for my big hunk of a man!"

He straightened his six foot four inch frame and she had expanded it ...just with a few words ... He felt ten foot tall.

"Anything you want to do to make yourself happy. I love the woman I fell in love with just the way you are. So don't change her for me." Then he kissed her on the nose as the door was being opened.

CHAPTER FIVE

Everyone came rushing to the door to greet them. It was like a stampede of cattle. Everyone then stopped and let Beatrice welcome them to their new home. Roscoe was beaming and standing beside her beaming.

"We have missed you so much! I will show James which room to put your bags in. You 'all just go on in and make yourselves comfortable," Roscoe said.

Madeline kissed him on the cheek and said, "My what an influence Beatrice has been on you, my dear boy." She smiled as Beatrice can over and hugged her.

She responded to grandma's comment, "Yes he has become a purrr-fect gentleman!"

"There she goes!" Roscoe thought to himself, "Purr means something else to Beatrice and him," and his face went beet red.

"Come this way James," waving to save himself any further embarrassment this time. That tall beautiful woman was going to pay for that but who's keeping score.

He returned and found Guy, "How is Kyleigh? Sorry I had to put the folks by your bedroom."

Roscoe was smiling. He was glad they weren't beside his bedroom. He didn't have the heart to tease Guy a bit.

It had been a stressful day and the girls did not know how stressful, that's the way the men wanted it.

"Question for everyone?" Roscoe was shouting.

He had all their attention and said, "You all want to eat out or have it catered here?" The vote was to cater and eat in.

Beatrice placed the order and announced it would be an hour for them to arrive and thirty minutes for them to set up the formal dining room.

"It will make it about 8:30 PM before we dine. If anyone wants to freshen up, or needs anything ... just ask Roscoe or me!" Beatrice said smiling.

Immediately she flitted off to find Kyleigh. That poor girl will be devastated when she finds out her house almost got blown up. Roscoe had told her that much, but not ALL had he told her.

He knew Beatrice may freak out if she saw a masked man with a Bruce face on it... Roscoe had two women that might freak out. So he looked upward for divine guidance.

Guy saw him and asked, "Something wrong with the ceiling, Bro?"

"Where is your wife?" Roscoe asked.

"With your wife," Guy frowned.

"You know they may both go off the deep end. Don't you?"

Roscoe was frowning. "That's why I was looking upward hoping this family could be spared ONE night to just enjoy each other before the storm comes."

"Roscoe we will be fine the danger is over," Guy was saying.

When Kyleigh came up, "What danger Guy?"

"The danger that grandma and Madeline may hear my wife screaming next door," he had to think of something fast.

"Bro the walls are soundproof. I promise, Kyleigh. If you want to make dumb butt here scream. Help yourself! You have my permission!" Roscoe bowed at her feet.

Kyleigh was holding her stomach, laughing so hard tears were running down her cheeks.

When Beatrice came up, Roscoe was still kneeling at Kyleigh's feet.

She asked, "Now why is my husband on bended knee and my best friend crying or laughing?"

Guy said, "I wanted him to instruct my wife on a few things," and gave Beatrice an exaggerated wink.

Roscoe said, "Now... dear I was just apologizing to Kyleigh for putting the folks beside them. I apologized on bended knee." Then he stood by his giraffe of a wife waiting for the volcano to erupt.

"My wife is a screamer," and chewed on the inside of his lip.

Beatrice said, "I know and Roscoe does ...very well!"

They were laughing so hard that Madeline wanted to join in. "What on earth on earth could you kids be talking about?"

"You ... grandma will be snooping all over Roscoe's new house looking for gadgets to make Trevor rise to the occasion!"

Madeline kissed her hand and slapped Guy hard on the back of his neck and said, "There's more where that came from!"

Trevor was bent over with laughter.

"I have sure missed my boys! You never know what will come out of their mouths!"

Guy looked at Roscoe, and Roscoe looked at Guy.

Madeline looked at both of them and said, "You two both had better not say out loud what you are thinking or I'll turn you across my knee.

Roscoe looked at his brother and said, "It ain't worth it!"

Guy said, "You're right her knees are getting bony!"

Madeline popped him in the back of his head again and said, "You two are grown men acting like BOYS! You'd better be glad the food is here."

Trevor said, "On the way over a few minutes ago ... I reminded her you 'all are not BOYS any more... and see what you have done. Y'all will be Madeline and my BOYS forever!" and he howled.

Whispering in Guy's ear, "That was a good distraction, Kyleigh looks happy, Bro!" Roscoe said.

Beatrice said, "Supper is on the table. Trevor will you say the blessing?"

"Of course my dear," they all bowed their heads and Trevor said the sweetest grace. Blessing his family. Blessing each couple. Thanking God for this new house and an extra blessing on his great grandbaby that is to be born! Let's eat!"

Halfway through the meal, the calm was gone.

One of the server spoke to Kyleigh, "I am so sorry about your house. You are in my prayers."

Kyleigh asked, "What are you talking about?"

The naive server said, "It's been all over the news," and he TOLD her.

Roscoe picked him up by the collar and walked him into the kitchen swinging in the air.

"What did I say?" he asked shakily.

Then they heard Kyleigh's blood-curdling scream.

"That's what you did! She did not know … so let this be a learning experience young man. Always ... always when serving keep your mouth shut!"

The screaming continued. The terrified young man nodded and ran out the backdoor.

Roscoe instructed the catering staff to clear the table and store the leftovers and desserts in their refrigerator. Then he turned to deal with the people on the other side of the kitchen door. "Thank goodness I had a nap," looking at the ceiling.

Beatrice had fainted. Trevor told Roscoe she was watching TV and they showed the mask of the Bruce man."

He told Madeline to get the emergency kit out of the bottom drawer in the kitchen on the right side of the sink.

"I will … that is right where I keep mine!" GM said.

"I need the smelling salts or ammonia!" Roscoe stated.

He picked her up and took her to their bed in their bedroom. Saying to himself, "It's a shame I have to wake her."

Madeline was back with the ampule of ammonia. It bought Beatrice back. She opened her pale green eyes and they fluttered. "What happened?" she asked rubbing her forehead.

"You fainted. Do you think you could already be pregnant?

It is a symptom … fainting that is ..." he was trying to distract her and it was working.

She was smiling and pulling him into bed with her.

He said, "Whoa! Whoa! BeBe honey. Whoa! We have a house full of guests."

That's when his face ashen again, and he sat her up. Then put her head between her legs. "It is suppose to prevent you from fainting again."

"Oh good, I was hoping it wasn't a new way to have sex."

He pulled her upright and said, "Really?" and then he pushed her head back down.

The doctor was in with Kyleigh and had given her a sedative. She was resting and Guy was sitting on the sofa across from her bed. Madeline was sitting by his side.

"Now that she knows, she will never go in our house."

"She has had a shock. All of those horrible flashbacks must be flooding her mind at once. This is normal for a victim as she. With this family's love … she will recover. Just give it time honey," GM was holding his hand and patting it.

"She was doing so well and she was so happy! You don't think this has hurt the baby?" Guy had a frightened look on his face.

"No dear ... God has a cocoon that protects them from far worse things … not to worry yourself about that. We are here for you and her. Trevor and I will not leave until she is better. You are not alone. Call me if you need me."

She went to her room where Trevor sat on their settee.

"How is she?" he was sipping a brandy that Roscoe had brought him.

"She is resting and Guy is exhausted. He is the one we need to worry about," she sat down beside him and he drew her into his arms to comfort her.

"Beatrice do you need anything?" Roscoe asked. She shook her head and nestled underneath the covers. The doctor had also given her a sedative.

"I'm going to see Guy for a few minutes. Now you rest my darling," she moaned and was asleep.

"Guy you okay, Bro?" Roscoe whispered as he entered their bedroom. He sat down beside a quiet haggard looking man that was his brother in all sense of the word.

"I'm fine … but she is not. She was so happy, Roscoe."

He began to sob. Roscoe put his hand on his shoulder and said, "I know how it was when Beatrice was in the hospital. I didn't think she would ever be the same. You were there for me and I am here for you. She will readjust with all the love around her. She is going to be fine in a couple of days. Get some rest. So you will be strong for her tomorrow. If you need me, just phone me. This house is too big for you to holler for me and the intercom may wake Beatrice up. Night!"

"Will do … night!" Guy said and Roscoe eased out the door.

The next morning Madeline and Trevor had gone out to the grocery store. So she could fix her boys, some breakfast. "A real breakfast," she said.

"If that's what will make mother hen happy, then let's do it!"

Trevor said, "But my lady, you don't have to! I can order," he pulled her ponytail.

"Hello Dolly NO! And have another server screw this day up! Nah, we are going to show our family what love is. Family Is. Is that clear! Oh wonderful man of mine!" looking up at him and batting those eyelashes.

She had her jeans on and those three inch heeled cowboy boots which made her six foot tall even. His six foot four height did not intimidate her one bit.

She made that clear as she was prancing into the kitchen with her husband … lugging in all the groceries.

Looking at him, "Well someone had to hold the door. Aren't I ... a good little doorstop?"

"Yes you are MY little doorstop and don't you forget, now that you are home. I think I will retire to my office," he went into Roscoe's library.

"It was better for him to say that than, "Cooking is woman's work" which he did only once. World War III was almost erupted on that day. He had learned to leave her to her area of expertise.

Roscoe had got the newspaper from the yard and was bringing it in. He saw the headlines and was glad he got it, instead of BeBe. Walking into the library, he saw Trevor sitting and he looked exhausted.

"Good morning, Are you okay?" Roscoe asked hanging onto the paper afraid he would lay it down.

"I've been to the grocery store with your grandmother and she dragged me all over that store. I didn't even know where they kept the bread. The only thing she wanted me to get. I bet I walked all over that store three times," he began rubbing his feet. "We left with my bedroom shoes on and I needed my walking shoes."

Roscoe wanted to burst out laughing but he didn't. He asked, "Did you think to ask someone?" "Real men don't ask for directions, boy!" Trevor laughed.

Roscoe let it rip, "It was just a loaf of bread, Trev!"

"It is the principle of it!" they were both cackling.

In walks Guy, "So what did I miss?"

"Trevor went with grandma to the grocery store," and he winked.

"Glad I missed that!" nodding his head.

Trevor asked Guy, "How is Kyleigh?"

"She's better. Beatrice is in with her. Roscoe... that wife of yours has a calming effect on my wife. Can we live here forever?" Guy said with those pleading puppy dog eyes. Those would always get him what he wanted.

"NO and I said NO! You always get your way about everything … but this I will draw the line. Come here, my dear brother," he had walked to the window.

Guy followed and Roscoe said firmly and pointed,

"See that beautiful house over there?"

"Yes... and your point is?" Guy said with a stone-face.

"That's … your damn house ... and that is where you WILL live …NOT here. Is that clear?" Roscoe stared back.

"Yep! As a bell!" and they started laughing their heads off.

Trevor said, "You 'all crack me up. Have you 'all been doing this long?"

"All our lives. We've been fighting over which bed, which covers, which toothbrush ... the list goes on. But this ... Guy paused. "But this one Roscoe wins! I concede dear brother, you are right! Come here a minute, Bro!"

Pointing through the window to his house... "That is where I'll be if you ever need me," Guy said.

Pointing to Guy's house, "See that house over there … That is where I will live … if BeBe should ever kick me out," and Roscoe squinted his eyes as if to see better.

Guy patted him on the back, "You can only visit … NOT live!"

Trevor was chuckling, when he hear his wife's voice as clear as a bell.

"When you two cutups get hungry ... food is on the table and bring your wives!" Madeline was barking.

"It's the intercom. One's in every room. So don't forget to shut them down at night!" Roscoe was laughing and winking at Trevor.

"We are on our way GM!" he told his grandmother over the intercom and then cut I off.

There was calm at breakfast. Kyleigh was looking out of the window in the kitchen sipping her juice. Beatrice was washing a few dishes and put the majority in the dishwasher.

Roscoe walked by to get more coffee and winked at Beatrice.

Kyleigh asked, "What was that all about?"

Beatrice grinned and Kyleigh begged her to tell.

"He wants to wash dishes," Beatrice put the sponge under the sink and batted her eyelashes at Kyleigh.

"You have got to be kidding!" Kyleigh's mouth was gaping.

"I'm training him right from the start. Yep! Your brother -in-law is going to clean every inch of this house."

Kyleigh still shaking her head as if to make the cobwebs leave it, and hopefully make sense out of what Beatrice was saying. She turned it to the side, and squinted her eyes and said simply, "Explain that!"

Beatrice walked to the refrigerator and picked out a peach, "Don't look so worried. I'm not going to make him a slave. Come let's walk around the pool and sit under the magnolia trees."

They had been friends for so long and they were completely opposites. The giraffe and the chipmunk sat laughing uncontrollably.

"You mean he wants sex the way you did it at the sink? OMG ... You may never get your dishes washed," Kyleigh said.

Beatrice smiled, "Yep! That's my boy. He is trying for twins. Hope it will be two little girls so I can duplicate them in frilly little pink lace dresses."

About then Guy and Roscoe walked around the corner with their coffee cups to join the girls.

"Correction! My little darling. If and when we should have twins ... they will be rambunctious little boys. What do you think, Bro?"

"I am staying far far out of the way on this one ... sounds like a tiff a brewing. What do you say K?"

Beatrice and Roscoe were glaring at each other like two bulls.

Kyleigh wiggled her maternity skinny jeans up close to Guy who was sitting in the glider.

"I think that is wise dear husband of mine," and giggled.

"Beatrice may I help you with the laundry?" Roscoe took her by the hand leading her to the laundry room ... still staring at each other as if they were mad.

Guy said, "He has lost his mind! He has never done laundry!" looking at Kyleigh with a puzzled look.

Kyleigh flipped the pages of her magazine and sipped her orange juice. Nonchalantly saying, "Don't worry about Roscoe. He is being well looked after ... and laundry is the last thing on those two's mind," continuing to flip pages faster.

"OH!" Guy was not slow and a grin started to appear on his lips. "I guess you want me to help you with our laundry?" staring into her eyes. She had had a bad night last night, but no flashbacks this morning.

She was the most beautiful girl in those damn skinny jeans. He took her hand and the book fell on the pool tiles. She rose on tip toe and kissed him, "No I want you to help me wash some dishes!"

"Trevor and Madeline are in the breakfast nook so dishes would have to wait," Guy saw her wiggling those skinny jeans and he added.

"I'll have James bring the limo and we can go to our new home and do the dishes there!" Guy proposed an alternative since he wanted her to want to go to their house. It was completely finished except for a little landscaping.

He was pushing her there. He added while he was holding her close and nibbling on her ear, "You don't have to. Just a thought."

"Call James quick I think Walmart is nearby. I need a few things," batting her eyelashes at him.

"NO dishes then, but shopping I am UP for," they were both getting hot at the thoughts of their wedding trip to Walmart.

This meant so much more ... never thought it could be any better.

He had definitely taught her how to please him and those words more, more, more ... were pounding in his temples until he could fulfill her wishes. Nothing would harm her again. He almost cried, his flashbacks of his innocent bride and that Banks, was unbearable. He quickly shook it away.

James drove them to their new home and she was smiling running from room to room.

"It is beautiful and just what I wanted. I will call Beatrice later and get my clothes. We can stay in our home. No more being ridiculous," he could feel her tremble.

"It's okay to talk it out. You promised to tell me how you feel," softly he said. Rubbing her back and squeezing her gluts to get her closer to him.

She had her arms around his neck, "As long as I have you by my side I will be fine," turning to look out at Beatrice and Roscoe's house.

After awhile and not looking at him she said, "I have to find a psychiatrist here. You told me to tell you my thoughts and I have my OB-GYN. I want to do everything right. This is our miracle baby!"

"You are so wise. It's the school teacher in you. You are teaching me. You have not told me what you want for the nursery?" Guy wanted her to know from day one where the baby's room would be. She had seen the building diagrams of it … now walking into the room. "It is perfect in every way."

Turning around and around so her husband would steady her. Which he did, grabbing her waist and leaning her back against his chest as they looked out the window at the mountains above and the lake below.

"Just like Beatrice and I talked about when we were little!"

Beatrice and Roscoe emerged from the laundry room in prim and proper attire.

She giggled, "That was close!" as they passed Madeline going in the laundry room for her clothes that she had folded earlier.

"Yes my dear! You are right!" Roscoe said as he walked toward Trevor to talk about sports.

"Twin girls is what I want," and he didn't even turn around to see her expression. He knew it was a grin and boy could that girl fold some laundry.

Trevor said, "What in the world is that smile all about?"

"Can't say! It is privileged information. If I tell, I put my life in danger!" Roscoe said stoically.

They both roared with laughter after Beatrice had gone to find Kyleigh.

"Madeline have you seen Kyleigh?" Beatrice asked with a puzzled expression.

"She left earlier in a big hurry. They didn't even say goodbye. Come here. Now look at that!"

Madeline was pointing to the white limo that was parked in Guy's front driveway.

"He has finally got his wife at home. I pray they can settle down. Guy has got to help out at the business. I have been pulling the load for him. I know that he has to be with Kyleigh at this time of adjustment to the house. Trevor and I are leaving this afternoon. We will be back for the party," still sipping her coffee.

"I'll tell her. I hope you rested well. Our door is always open to you guys," hugging Roscoe as he and Trevor came into the room.

"Slept like a baby and Trevor snored like an old man!" Madeline teased.

Trevor popped her on her rear.

"Not in front of the children dear!" Madeline straightened to her tallest height and looked Trevor in the eyes.

Trevor was fixing to say why he had slept so soundly was because Madeline had had her way with him all night.

He chuckled and was going to ring for a cab.

Roscoe said, "No way are you going by cab. We are taking the Silverado."

"OK, Son! I've been wanting to ride in it!" Trevor helped Madeline into the back seat, and Roscoe helped Beatrice into the back seat.

Off to the airport they went. At the airport one of Trevor's friends was patting him on the back.

Saying he was, "Sorry to hear about Jeff Saunders being a smuggler and shooting your daughter-in-law instead of the masked man that was protecting her."

Madeline was holding Beatrice up until Roscoe could pick her up and take her back to the truck. They had said a quick good-bye and Madeline's eyes was saying "I am so so sorry!"

Roscoe and Beatrice had returned home in silence.

Beatrice entered the kitchen. "So this sniper shot me … and killed this masked man I was afraid of. He was an innocent man. How we misjudged him? You knew?"

"I knew... Trevor told me earlier. We didn't want to upset you. I didn't want to make Trevor feel any worse than he already did. He was devastated after his other friend Lance followed Jeff." Roscoe was now looking at the mountaintop and watching the sun set, an orange horizon going slowly down. He did not want Beatrice to see the blood in his eyes. He could kill Jeff with his bare hands for what he had done to his wife. Then he heard Beatrice in the bathroom throwing up.

He caught her around her waist before she went limp.

This is the second time, she has fainted. Now this woman is going to the doctor and have a pregnancy test done. He could hardly contain himself. He was so happy.

Beatrice awoke and asked, "What have you been doing?" "Nothing dear, just made you an appointment with the doctor for a PG test. That okay with you?" Roscoe began grinning like a opossum.

"Did I faint again?" wide-eyed Beatrice was looking at him.

"Yep! And puked, too!" Roscoe announced.

They were both smiling like opossums at the medical office, when the next day the doctor confirmed she was indeed pregnant.

Guy and Kyleigh got a call from Roscoe saying for them both to come to Roscoe's house quickly.

They rushed into the kitchen which was the quickest way to get in. "What's wrong Bro?" holding Kyleigh's hand for support. The way things had been going lately they thought it was something bad when …

"Beatrice and I …" Beatrice ran to the bathroom and vomited. Roscoe was with her so was Guy and Kyleigh.

Beatrice said to Kyleigh, "You are the lucky one!"

"What are you talking about?"

"You don't have to puke your guts out for three months." and she threw up again.

Roscoe was being hugged by Guy and patted on the back and then chest bumped, "Congrats, Bro!"

Kyleigh was down on her knees wiping the perspiration from Beatrice's brow, "You know what this means?"

"Yep we are going to have children together around March!" burping and puking, laughing and hugging. They had been through so many times, caring for each other when sick. It was normal sitting on the bathroom floor talking.

The guys had found some beers and were sitting in the huge den watching football. Beatrice said, "It's a good thing you came Kyleigh. Roscoe would have left me in the bathroom to die alone!"

Roscoe rose and recited a prepared oration, "No, dear! I would not have! ... I am told that comes with the second child and you two were laughing so hard. I knew you were in good hands."

They all four raised their right hand in a fist, "Rah Rah Rah Team!" like they did in grammar grades on the football field.

Immediately Beatrice flew to the bathroom. Roscoe went behind her this time. She was so pitiful. The doctor said, "he could come and give you a shot? But you must replace those fluids you lost … can I get you some ginger ale?" she threw a wet washcloth at him.

"Call him NOW!" she barked as her eyes were bulging.

"What a difference a day can make!" Roscoe thought.

"This is no damn picnic, so you had better not go and watch football … I want you to be with me every step of the way!" those beautiful pale green eyes were drawing him down to the floor. "I will I promise," he said.

"You want to clean the toilet?"she asked. "Yeah Yeah yeah," he panted. "Then scrub it. Don't come near me. Really scrub!"

CHAPTER SEVEN

Trevor and John got the luggage out of the long white limo while Madeline was inside rubbing Smokey Joe. He was glad they were home. The cat never showed them affection except when they had been gone for this long. He would sleep in their bed tonight.

Trevor said, “I’ve got to get that cat a bed of his own.”

“Pay no attention to Trev, darling! You are my little man,” and the cat was purring as loud as a motorboat.

“Trev is my big man … You understand? Of course, you do!” Madeline cooed.

“You talk to that cat like he knows what you are saying,” walking to the bedroom for the third time, frowning each time.

“He does … He has for ten years … Been one of my life savers!” smiling and batting her eyelashes at Trevor.

“I admit I am jealous of that damn cat! You rub him, you caress him and say sweet nothings into his ears,” Trevor pouted.

“You are jealous… I didn’t see that one coming! But tonight he will not be in here … so I will do all those things to you!”

He was a macho man and all of a sudden, he picked her up and walked to the room next door.

"Let SJ have his room. You and I are going to take a ride around the world next door!" and they did.

He would always be her hero. This man was her soulmate and had waited for her for so long … as she had for him.

"Smokey Joe told me … he wanted to go home," she looked at the mirror as she brushed her hair.

"Are you sure? Are do you want to go home? I wish you could settle here, but now I want to go home, too! To your home. The boys are there," he paused.

She had not said a word.

He kissed her ponytail and said, "I'll start working on it tomorrow. You can text me where you want your new house to be. You better specify what you want in it or I'll have steers meeting you at the door. If you want it just like this one …that would save me a heap of trouble."

"I want it just like this one … because this is your home. It's just in the wrong state … and in the wrong town. The new house will be our new home." She kissed him and opened the door for Smokey Joe who bounced up on the bed beside Trevor and purred.

He looked at the cat and said, "Don't you know you live in the next room," all the while rubbing the cat's silver coat.

"OK cat! I will walk you to your room. I mean my room."

Madeline smiled and waved, if she spoke to either, the other would get jealous.

Trevor had Beatrice and Kyleigh's dogs delivered with a trainer to instruct the dogs for a week. He wanted the girls to feel safe while the boys were at work.

Kyleigh was thrilled to see her Black Velvet .They had grown a lot since she saw them in Dallas.

Beatrice was taken aback with Dynamite. It was the most beautiful dog that she had ever seen. Roscoe had had to help her adjust because of her morning sickness.

She told her Dynamite, "This too shall come to pass!" and kissed her dog on the head. Roscoe said, "Hey! What about me?"

The trainer was laughing so hard, "I do have to show you the button."

Roscoe looked at Beatrice and simultaneously asked, "What button?" They were outdoors and she said, "Come inside and I will show you. This is a safety button for you. If the dog cannot handle a situation he will run and press it… the police, SBI and FBI will be alerted and will be on there way. This is Trevor's wedding gift to you."

Roscoe hugged Beatrice and the dog sat very still.

The trainer said, "You have to be careful how you hug her, sir!"

Roscoe said, "I know I haven't got used to her being pregnant, yet!" He rubbed her stomach and talked to the baby.

The trainer said, "That is not what I meant. Your dog has been trained to attack anyone who holds Beatrice down and she screams. The dog will tear them to bits. He will do the same for you, too. You are both his masters.'

Roscoe looked at Beatrice and Roscoe looked at her and they said together, "We are going to be in a heap of trouble."

The trainer asked, "What do you mean?"

Beatrice shook her head, "You tell her!"

"Well let me see how I can put this delicately. We have

a screamer in the house. She only screams when she has a orgasm. There it is. What do we do? Because I am always holding her down...."

All the while he is rubbing the dog's head affectionately and trying not to look at the female trainer in the eyes. All he wanted was to hear what she had to say.

"I understand. Put her in her crate and set the timer. The dog when she hears the ticking, will be calm and put a sock in your wife's mouth."

Roscoe and Beatrice couldn't believe what they were hearing.

"I was kidding! Just kidding! I like to lighten it up every now and then. My dry humor gets me in trouble with Trevor sometimes. They have the same problem!"

Roscoe face was so red, Beatrice grabbed his arm. "It's her humor honey! That's all it is! Miss Adams You are talking about his grandmother. He is like our new dog, he would kill for her."

"Is the other grandson the same way?" the trainer asked. "I got to go over there next!" Roscoe said, "He is worse than me! No GAG jokes! If you value YOUR life!"

Guy and Kyleigh did not know about the button or the screaming. So now that the dogs were settled, the trainer left.

She returned every day for a week and put the dogs through their exercises and the owners through theirs.

Dynamite & Velvet were a happy relief. They had begun to walk every day for the OB-GYN had said it was the best exercise, but Guy and Roscoe thought they had a better idea of how they should exercise. They told the girls it every day.

Guy had asked the trainer on the last day, if she could

return on the 20th of August, because they were having a huge party and did not want the dogs to get upset. We are having it at our house. It is to be over one hundred people attending.

You can keep the dogs at Roscoe and Beatrice's. She agreed to return that day, and anytime day or night. "Feel free to use our services. Here is my card!"

Kyleigh looked at Guy, "This is a good thing. Out dog will be really trained by March and can protect our little bundle of joy … I know the guards are outside, but Black Velvet will be with us inside. That makes me very happy!"

"I will tell Trevor that the first chance I get or do you want to on the 20th?"

He wanted her to continue to feel safe. She was amazing. She had first thought of the baby and then herself.

"You can text him. It will make his day. He told me you boys never text me only Madeline. So go for it Babe!" blowing him a kiss and scooting into the den with the dog bouncing behind her.

"Beatrice called," Roscoe said, "but she had to go throw up, so I told him you would call her back in a few."

"I do feel for her, but I am so glad I don't have to go through that!" Kyleigh said and Guy was nodding his head.

"Hey, Beatrice what are you doing?" Kyleigh said as if she didn't know.

"I am barfing all over my gorgeous new Dynamite," Beatrice moaned. "I wanted to go over the invitation list with you."

Kyleigh said, "We can do it tomorrow when you feel better!"

"I may still be in the same fix … so shoot! Meet me at

the pool in a few. I'll bring my plastic bag. It is saving these beautiful floors, but I don't want to mess up your digs!"

"You come over. No worries!" she was looking out the window when saw a man in a masked man that looked like Bruce. "Don't come BeBe! Don't come!"

"Why? And you had better tell me!" Beatrice knew her friend well and sometime was up.

"There is a mask man outside of our house..." she said in a shaky voice. "I can't scream or the dog will go berserk!"

"You are right … Don't scream! The man is protecting you! I found out ..." and she proceeded to tell her about Jeff.

"Guy is in big trouble! He should have told me not you!"

"Samuel Steven Smith III come right here and explain!"

Guy heard that as he shuffled quickly back out of the den.

"Beatrice I will call you back. I have a bone to pick with my husband," patting her little foot on the floor.

"I understand and tomorrow will be better. Toodles!" she hung up and told Roscoe not to go anywhere near his brother's house tonight.

"Why?"

"The roof may fly off!"

"You need to explain that! It sounds serious?" his brows were furrowed and his fists were clenching.

"Kyleigh is fuming as I was .. because Guy did not tell her about those ninjas around the house. I feel good about them now. The point is dear husband of mine. We females need to know these things, too. So they don't freak us out." Beatrice stopped and asked. "Are you listening?"

Roscoe had been extremely quiet through her lecture.

He had learned long time ago not to interrupt an angry

woman. On the force before an interrogation where the woman was handcuffed. Let her rant …

"Handcuffed," his gears had switched. "Where are my handcuffs, dear?"

"Don't you change the subject! Don't you dare! The dog will tear you to shreds!" He was walking toward her and stepped over the dog to get to her.

Holding her loosely he said, "You and those pale green eyes need to be handcuffed to our bed in three minutes. Is that clear?" she nodded.

"I will secure the dog and set the timer … your nausea shot will wear off in an hour so hop to it woman!" gently patting her buttocks where he use to swat them.

And the race was on and he promised to never keep anything from her as she lay there naked spread eagle in their bed.

"Tell me what else you want me to do for you?" he was straining to remain in control.

She had her long legs twisting and twisting and she did till she said, "I want it now! Now!" pursing her lips as tight as she could so she would not make a sound.

He covered her mouth to stifle her screams …over and over.

Never did he let his lips come off of hers.

It was perfect timing. The timer dinged!

He quickly took the handcuffs off and stood looking to see her satisfied face that mouthed, "I love you!"

He had let the dog out, sat down watching the game and rubbing the dog's head. "Next year the baby will be watching it with us, correction babies," talking to himself.

"When BeBe has questions I have to answer in the

future, I will think of this night!" continuing to embed this into his memory.

His security guards had been informed to leave the masked men with Bruce's face alone that they maybe on his property or Guy's property from time to time.

He told them if they are around, then something was up.

He just hoped it wasn't the calm before the storm.

He was cool as a cucumber, listening to the dog whining while Beatrice threw up in the downstairs bathroom.

CHAPTER EIGHT

Bruce had a mission to clear his name. From his cell, he had finally found his father's murderer, THE SHERIFF. He could see the smirk on the sheriff's face. The sheriff had helped a kingpin by the name of Foo Mao Jung in Japan to supply Banks with cocaine. He used Chris Shackleford to blow up his father's plane.

Bruce had sent his men to protect Guy and his grandson.

As he listened to Unitus snore night after night, he thought of Jana. He knew she had gone back to Japan and would not be back. She always obeyed her husband.

He ached for her. He loved her like no other, but he had screwed up. He should have told her he was undercover.

Then she probably would not have believed him, she knew all of her operatives, but not his.

He dozed for ten minutes and Jana was there . Only in his dream. He shook his head vigorously, to make the torment stop.

Unitus said from his side of the cell, "Man stop! You are going to make yourself pass out. I ain't picking you up. I'll just piss on you!" and laughed so all the inmates were telling them to shut the F--- up!

"Piss away. I'll have a better view to cut your balls off.

Make no mistake … you would never use that pisser again!" He spoke softer, but all could hear. Then he shook the bed. Not because he was scared but because he wanted him to try. It was to let Bruce know he had heard what he said ... and he would be ready.

Unitus looked forward out through the iron bars … this burly 350 lb six foot tall muscular beast … hollered into the abyss.

"It would be my pleasure to disassemble you ... piece by piece" … timing his words slowly …"If you don't shut up so these men can sleep, that is exactly what I will do!" growling like a mad grizzly bear.

The ground work had been set from day one. This was Bruce's undercover man and he was a professional body builder, also. He walked through the crowd, and it parted.

In the prison system that was very rare. All cliches admired Unitus's workouts. They would say, "Ain't messing with him for nobody!" Others would say, "That's what mom warned me about DON'T DROP THE SOAP around this one," and the crowd would roar with laughter ... until Unitus stood up and then you couldn't hear a pin drop.

Bruce was secure for the time being … but he was no fool.

Trust no one … had saved his life a many of times, and that is why, he slept like he did. This was one of those night's that Jana's face would not leave him alone.

Jana was in her cocoon at her parent's house. She felt as if her heart had been ripped out when Bruce told her not to come back.

She had heard about Jeff Saunders and his scheming and

treason. It had not set well with her that Bruce had supplied Banks with cocaine. Then Banks was selling it to a PTSD veteran that had served his country well. Now he served his drug habit, mainly because of her husband.

Bruce had never in all these years let Jana see this side of him. He was a perfect gentleman around her and he lavished her with tender affection and lavished her with expensive gifts to make her happy. "Nothing was too good for his Jana," she remembered him saying.

He was so good. That was all she saw. Why did he do it? She could not wrap her head around it. It just made no sense to her. His own mother, Madeline hated him. That's what she knew because he had told her that one true statement long, long ago.

She would have loved to have a case like this to solve when she was in the CIA, but now she had resigned her job. She would not go back to that kind of life. She had a fear her husband would be killed at any moment and she did not want to be in the middle.

That was the real reason she had come home. She could not bear to see the love of her life be murdered. She knew what kind of people he associated with, and it would not be pretty.

She cried into her pillow every night.

Her mother did not know. "Where is your husband? I don't understand your Brucie. He is always here when you are. Do you want to talk to your mother?"

She would always shake her head, "No mother. Not yet!"

And to herself, "No mother never!"

Her father came in one day and said that their cousin

had been killed in the states. He added two other cousins in the same kind of work were still in the states.

"We will pray for them. They work for Bruce so they will be fine. Let us pray!"

They sat together and she sipped her sake and asked her father, "Did you say they work for Bruce now?"

"Yes, dear. He needed them and they went months ago. Men DON'T always tell their wives everything!" he patted her hand that lay on the table.

"What have you not told mother?" she queried to see him squirm. They laughed together. It felt good. Father and daughter had always been close and he had to hide many things from his wife an Jana knew it.

That night Jana lay in her bed and ached for her husband and her father's words loomed from her dream... "Men don't always tell their wife everything" ...

She woke drenched in sweat and tears running down her cheeks.

Had Bruce not told her everything? ... Like I love you ... Was he trying to protect her? That would be just like her Bruce. Her mother's Brucie ... the sweet loveable man that she had married till death do us part!

Jana had requested three times for her conjugal visit with her husband. Bruce had denied her three times. He had to deny her again. It was killing him inside.

As he walked through the door ... he had been prepared to hurt her and send her away. "I told you not to come back."

Her perfume was his favorite ... the dress was a kimono that he had had specially designed for her with white and pink cherry blossoms that hugged her magnificent figure of porcelain white. He closed his eyes and remembered their honeymoon under the cherry blossoms.

He opened his eyes... "I told you not to come back!"

She had pulled out all the stops but one! She walked up to him and grabbed his privates and kneaded them. He swallowed and bent over her. He was gone.

Every fiber in him was magnifying his hunger and it's intensity grew and grew till she thought she or he would not make it to live another day. She bit his naked shoulder, he suckled her neck as the upper half was functioning but the bottom half was frozen together … pulsating ...neither wanted it to stop and neither would finish without the other … always had been that way. "God I have missed you" he said. She squeezed him with a spasm and arched, "Show me how much you missed me." He lowered her and her body was still wrapped intact around him. He went slow … it was killing him. She was speeding up and slowly went limp … then ooh yes! and the aah yes! ... in his ear that she bit. "Go baby Go baby and when you can't go any more! ... I will finish for you!

"The hell you say! Jana... Jana … Jana!" He yelled so loud the entire complex knew her name.

In one hour... they had devoured each other in so many many ways … and neither would ever forget this day!

When she left she said, "Don't you dare say it! I will say it! .... I will be back!" and she left.

When he returned to his cell, Unitus looked at him and did not comment. He slept the entire night.

The next day Jana began her search for the answers, even if it killed her. She did not have the CIA coverage, she was on her own. Something was brewing and in Dallas, she had friends there. She was going to call in some favors. Her first stop was the library. It was huge. She could go online but it could be traced. No one followed her to the library. These days of technology … nah!

It was not done by grownups. So she was in disguise as an older teenager that was going to college, and had a backpack as a purse.

She found everything about the Smith Oil Refineries' plane crash. She had xeroxed everything she could ... news coverages ... periodicals that had editorials opinions, etc.

This was just her beginning point. As she walked back to her car, she saw a ninja with Bruce' face on the mask … that took every step she took. That meant Bruce still love her. Boy did he love her. She was still tingling from yesterday!

"Jana so good to see you!" Madeline was rising from her desk to give her daughter-in-law a hug.

"I thought you were in Japan?"

Jana smiled and asked, "Is this room still bug proof?"

Madeline walked to the door and locked it and turned the intercom completely off.

"Now shoot! What's going on?" Madeline was puzzled.

Jana began, "You know that women have intuitions which tend to be a pain sometimes!" Madeline nodded.

"Well my mother said something and my father, also. Now I am here. I love your son!" Madeline bristled but said nothing.

"And he loves me even though he told me to go to Japan and never come back … he did that to protect me. Now I have found out through another operative that he has been indeed undercover ... Bruce since his father was killed has been working to find out who did it!"

Madeline's eyes were dilating, but she said nothing.

Jana continued, "Since he has been in jail … he has sent my cousins to protect Guy and his grandson. Now as I look over my shoulder there is one of his men here to protect me."

"Will you help me get him out?" she begged.

"The Jared Banks thing can be self- defense," she stated.

"I have to have my husband back, the soft gentle husband I had in Japan," a tear fell into Jana's hand.

"I want him to see his family …. because all my family ... love him dearly!"

"One of the main reasons I am here is ... I have no coverage NO longer covered by the CIA …" she paused.

"Yes, I am on my own, but I will fight for him! Alone if I have too!" she stated.

"Will you help me? I beg of you ... your SON is worth it!"

She could say no more. Her heart ... she had poured out.

Every ounce of her being was waiting for Madeline's answer.

PART SIX

CHAPTER ONE

Tate Shackleford had settled into his Aunt Eunice's home of four kids. They were brats. Tate had seen how she catered to their every need.

He'd had to fight for what he got. Adam, he saw on TV was in jail waiting for trial. So he might as well make the best of it until something better comes along.

The oldest of his cousins was Jennifer, a real brainac. She always had her head in a book. Eighteen years old, but the mindset of a preteen. He laughed at his assessment of her. Then he admitted he wished he loved books like she did. Maybe she would help him with his schoolwork.

He was always looking for an angle of how to use people that befriended him.

Then there was Coraine the sixteen year old hippie-dippie.

She could care less about school. She just went to pick up boys to skip school with. He was not going near that fruitcake. He saw the weed in her jean jacket. He just hoped his new home, didn't get raided because he would be out on the street. He may have to rat her out to Aunt Eunice to save her family from public humiliation.

he laughed to himself as he was unpacking the paper bag of his clothes. He knew public degrading of a child. He was the post child because of his uncle Chris and his brother Adam.

He had it all stored in the closet of the two boys room.

They had bunk beds and his aunt had put him on an air mattress on the floor. She said, if it worked out she would buy him a single bed, soon as she could.

The thirteen year old boy's name was Corey. Who named a boy... a girl's name? He was into skateboarding and had told him he could hang out, if he bought a skateboard. With what? He had nada money.

Then there was the nine year old boy named Jason. Auntie said she named him after Jason Bourne. He was a tattletale. Yep, an out and out pain in the crack.

"You know Matt Damon's character. Don't you go to the movies?"

"Nah, we had to have food that was a little more important.

Adam said he was going to get a better job and then we could go to the movies ... but he never did," Tate admitted.

"Yeah he wants me to keep you in school. That was his only request. He does love you Tate. He knew I would take you in. He saw the handwriting on the wall. I am going to be upfront with you and you can take it anyway you like."

"I like in your face honesty. I have had enough bull sh--- to last a life time," Tate said.

"Adam and you are Chris Shackleford's sons. Adam didn't have the guts to tell you. He left the dirty work up to me. You can either put your nose to the books and make something out of yourself ... or end up like them two! What 'll it be?" hands on her hips.

She looked like a drill sergeant standing there over top of him. He had thought he was tough but this news had hit him square in the stomach and he had buckled.

"I will do whatever you say, but first I need a hammer and a box of nails. Do you have a sturdy fence?"

"Yeah … what you got in mind? NO I don't have a dog. Just a sign." She got him the hammer and nails. "Here you go? Can I watch? Don't want anything damaged." She followed him out to the fence that she had pointed to.

He was not one for crying, but he had known a man one time that told him this … that he was about to do.

"Son if you ever get angry enough to want to hurt someone or destroy someone's property ... go get a hammer and drive as many nails as you can pound into a fence ... and then pull everyone of them out. By the time you get them all out your anger will be subsided and where you can manage it." Tate spit on the ground and continued talking to his aunt.

"He said when the man was a kid, he hammered 100 nails and by the time he got the last ten out ... he could hardly walk to the house. He said never do a hundred or your arms will hurt for a week!" Tate laughed.

Tate had never forgot that as he told Aunt Eunice.

"I'm real mad so I'll be hammering for awhile," he said.

"I understand. Help yourself. I'll be cooking some supper," and she walked to the house. If the neighbors complained, she'd deal with them. That boy needed to do a powerful lot of hammering.

Eunice's church had rallied around her when her husband was killed while overseas. Her military family as well, had helped her and the kids through the initial grieving period.

She had never worked publicly until then. She took a receptionist position at a law firm. The children had always been her first priority. They would always be a part of Roger, her husband. She would try her best to do what he would want her to do for the kids.

As she was washing dishes, she looked out the window at Tate getting his anger out. She promised herself she would one day, do some hammering of her own.

She had a lot of anger after losing her best friend . Her husband Roger had been her everything and now he was gone.

She just hoped that fence that Roger put up would stand for awhile longer for Tate and her to give it a pounding.

The children had eaten and Tate was still pulling out nails.

She would fix him a plate for later.

When he did come in, they all hugged him ... one at a time.

This was the weirdest, he had ever felt. No one ever hugged him unless they wanted something.

Lastly his aunt said, "Welcome to the family Tate. You are one of us from this day forward."

Jennifer said, "Tate in a few months, I'll be going off to college and you can have my room. Just wanted you to have first dibs at it. Mother agreed the boys had been too mean to get it." They made faces at their sister.

Coraine told Jennifer,"When you leave I am outta here, too!"

Aunt Eunice asked, "And just where do you think you are going young lady?"

"To the moon!" and walked off. She was trying her

mother's patience, but she would deal with the sixteen year old later.

The two boys, Corey and Jason were too busy high-fiving him and that is how the first day went. It was his first glimpse of a real family.

It was new and he admitted, he felt loved. He was going to give it his best shot. His arms ached.

Roscoe was back to work and he wanted to stay there for three months until the morning sickness went away. He laughed at himself, "You got what you asked for."

The security guards were giving him a fit. Every day there was something on his desk. A baby bottle, a baby rattle, a single diaper just to name a few .... then came the handcuffs, the ball and chain, etc. They are having a field day.

At his next meeting he said, "I am so proud of you' all. You have truly showed teamwork and camaraderie in the last few weeks … Now I would like to use it in your job descriptions. There are a list on the front of your applications." The room got quiet.

He continued, "I am proud of the nice job you have been doing protecting my family. I wanted to give you a heads up on the 20th of this month, we are having a massive house-warming party for my brother, Guy and his wife, Kyleigh. I will be needing all the volunteers that want to do overtime, because I want the place to have double coverage. Not expecting trouble, but best be prepared."

"Are there any questions?"

"Then I shall retire to the nursery," and he walked into his office. They all sat and looked at one another.

"Ouch!" Inscoe said. "We got to lighten up fellows. He

is buckling under pressure. It's the Mrs.'s barfing that he can't handle. Not us! He has always been able to handle us!" They all nodded and went back to work.

Beatrice had her plastic bag at Kyleigh's pool and the two dogs were playing on the grass.

"Okay where was I? You lucky person. Who else do you want to invite? Madeline sent this … getting out her phone to read the text … PLEASE invite my friends … Jackie, Sophie and a man named Lefty ... she has all their last names and addresses listed. She said the weirdest thing that Guy would know them all because they had helped you 'all. Don't know them myself."

"Me either, but if Madeline wanted them and they know my sweetie, we will definitely include them. So that should be the last of them. Unless you can think of anyone else?" K said.

"My mother said she was coming over to rub my brow, so I will be off. Come Dynamite! We must go and see grandma. I just hope she doesn't hold me down and scream when she see my dog. Wish me luck!" waving bye.

Kyleigh picked up the basket and called Black Velvet one time and she was there. She patted her head and told her what a good girl she was. They had become inseparable. She had never been allowed to have a pet in the house while growing up.

Her mother was too particular about the Middleton house. "I will have no mongrel strewing hair all over the place. That is THAT!" Kyleigh giggled and went inside.

She reached down and patted her head again and said, "You just strew all you want to . You are my baby now!" screwing her mouth up like she was cooing to a baby.

Guy came in out of the den saying, "And I thought I was your only baby?" raising one brow. "Now I see I have competition! It's a good thing I have to work today or I would give that dog a piece of my mind. Did you finish the list?"

She was putting the lavender flowers into a vase and arranging them at the sink while wiggling ... wiggle, wiggle, wiggle. She had her purple skinny jeans on, would he notice?

About that time he kissed her bare shoulder, her blouse was one of those off the shoulder styles. "I have told you about those jeans ..."

"And I've told you the dog will get you so go to work," and she was wiggling and giggling all the way to the den with the flowers and her dog was taking every step she took.

Guy was talking to Madeline and was talking way too fast. All he could think of was those lavender skinny jeans.

"Guy are you listening to me!" GM asked.

"No ma'am, I will have to call you back!" GS said.

He was whistling for the dog and pointing to the crate. The timer was set. He was on to someone playing opossum and picked her up and laid her gently on the bed.

Her eyes opened like a deer in headlights.

"How many pairs did you order?" he asked.

"Only one for every day of the week . Is that too much for you?"

"OH NO you didn't say that! You will pay for that my lovely wife because next year we will not have the chance, and I may give out by then. Your pregnancy has made you horny as hell . . . and I love it!" He had her out of those jeans and she did not have time to wiggle.

"Ding!" He ran for the crate and she ran for the shower.

"Boy can she scream and you did not hear a thing! Did you Velvet?" and he was rubbing her behind her ears.

"Let's go to work! I'll race you!" he and the dog ran.

"Aren't you tired yet?" Kyleigh was looking at Guy.

"Never I have six more ... six days. You had better be napping. I don't want to tire the baby out!" he said.

"Never I have six more days of bliss!" and walked out of his office only because Velvet was there.

She hollered, "That dog saved you. Give her a treat!"

All he could do was go back to work. That dog had her eyes on him. He was now a prisoner to work and his warden had four legs.

So he let the dog out of the den to go find her master and keep her safe. He was definitely grateful to Trevor for the dog. She was perfect for Kyleigh.

She had told him how safe she felt and she was talking to him about everything. She was also keeping her doctor appointments and they had been to one NAMI meeting.

She was a teacher and she was teaching him about mental health. She was an amazing woman.

CHAPTER TWO

Trevor saw that Madeline was wearing a sad face, so he thought he would put a smile on it.

He took her to the balcony outside and they stared at the full moon and the breeze blew her ponytail over his shoulder.

He took a deep breath of her Jasmine perfume.

"Mmm you smell delightful my darling!"

She turned and pecked his cheek.

"I have something to ask you and I want you to be thinking about this for awhile. Then give me an answer."

"You are killing me with suspense. What could you possibly be up to, now?" they sat down on the glider with flowery plush pillows.

"You miss the boys don't you?"

"Yeah … I do!" dropping her lashes so he could not see how much.

"How would you like it, if we move back home?"

Her eyes widened and her mouth flew open, "You can't be serious?" trying not to be so happy. That would hurt him, if she did not want to live here in his home. He said, "I am very serious," she looked straight into his eyes.

"I also miss the boys!" and kissed her lips softly.

"And you are not going to be happy not seeing our new grandchildren when they are born. Only now and then won't cut it!" he added.

"I agree that would make me sad. So what are you thinking about for us?" Madeline asked.

He said, "We will build in Hendersonville ... a mansion of your choice, my dear. With all the bells and whistles!"

"But you love it here?" she looked worried.

"We can build this same house there!" looking at her for her reaction.

"OH Trev! That would be the best of both worlds to me. I know you would not be happy anywhere else but here ... then you just pull out the solution right out of thin air!"

She was kissing him all over his face.

He said, "WOW I should have said that while we were inside. The guards are watching!"

She took him by the hand and lead him inside and kissed him so good that it curled the toes on his ostrich skin cowboy boots.

"You are making it too easy for me," he said.

"I beg your pardon!" she stared at him questioning what he just said.

He squared off with her, "Just what I said!" grabbing her waist.

She was definitely getting riled, "Easy?"

"I thought I was going to have to listen to a list of decor that you wanted in a mansion that I probably wouldn't like. Yeah! Easy!" laughed and continued holding her.

"Easy for me to call Roscoe and have him find a contractor," adjusting his grip on her because she was wiggling.

"Easy this place I have the floor plans and landscape designs tucked away in my safe!" Trevor was smiling.

"OK! I'm EASY! I wouldn't change anything about it. I know you love it here. If you are happy, I am happy!" GM batted her eyelashes and sealed the deal in the bedroom.

He called Roscoe and told him he would fax him the plans and if there were any questions by the contractor, he would pay for his flight and travel expenses to look at Southfork."

He paused and she was nodding and waving for him to continue.

"She wants it down by the lake and around the curve from her sweet boys! You get the acreage layout and when we come for the housewarming party, I will sign the papers."

"And another thing ... don't let those girls scream while the dogs are around. You all four go to dinner on me and tell them there, so the restaurant can throw you out. I will say to GM, it is all her fault!" Looking at Madeline who no longer, had a sad face.

She had a satisfied glow in her red negligee that was sheer at all the right places. He was a lucky Texan and he knew it!

The guests were arriving for the long awaited house-warming party and no detail was left unnoticed. They had hired a valet parking crew to park the cars and let the guests off at the door.

There they were greeted by their new butler, Henri and new maid, Agnes. She was to circulate and see if anyone needed anything with her crew keeping the house sparkling.

Their were two bartenders, one inside and one by the swimming pool where there was a Tuscany full outdoor kitchen. Also the pool had a two dolphin fountain that was lit and flowing into the pool.

The band outside was "rock and roll" themed, while inside by the black baby grand piano was the three stringed ensemble of violin, cello, and piano playing softly "Bach and Beethoven" which both Beatrice and Kyleigh loved them.

The catering service had arrived two hours prior to set up.

HORS d` OEUVRES: Shrimp/ Lobster/ Beef/ Chicken/ Steak and Ham combination: sliced/ chopped/ minced
Crackers: Rye/ Wheat/ Pumpernickel/ Saltine/ Ritz
Fruits: Strawberries/ Cherries/ Pineapple/ Apple/ Mango
Designer cookie cup with ice cream or whipped cream
Vegetable Sticks: Carrots/ Celery/ Scallions/ Broccoli
Cheeses: American/ Brie/ Gouda/ Provolone/ Sharp Cheddar/ Pepper Jack

In the huge dining room at the center of the table was a lit ice sculpture with two more dolphins carved into the ice.

Champagne flutes, and cocktails were on trays and being offered throughout the rooms.

At the centre were two beautiful women Beatrice and Kyleigh. They were dressed in designer maternity frocks that Beatrice's mother had made. Everyone was commenting on how amazing, they were done. She was being commissioned to make a woman's daughter … a wedding dress and another wanted ... two cocktail dresses for special events.

BeBe's mom was so happy as well as her father. He loved the tailoring business as much as she. This could be the start of their new venture.

Kyleigh and Beatrice were the only two that had ginger ale.

Their husbands were probably the only two not imbibing into the hard stuff. The girls said, "If we can't ... you can't! It's about being equals on this pregnancy journey!"

Guy kissed Kyleigh, and Roscoe kissed Beatrice. Immediately Beatrice had Roscoe by the hand leading him through the house to the back elevator and pressed the stop button, after they got in. She stood as close to him as she could without touching him.

The sheer dress was silky and when it rubbed, it made her nipples hard. They bumped Roscoe's chest every time she took a deep breath. Her gorgeous pale green eyes were looking into his eyes.

"The way I see it, we have two glorious hours before my injection wears off. Do you want to waste this time or not? The trainer is watching the dogs. The party is large enough that no one will miss us for a few."

He was nodding yes and she began pulling his handkerchief from his suit pocket, ever so slowly like she had done his tie at the wedding. Then she took off her thong panties and he place them in his pant's pocket that was growing in size. Roscoe was quivering. She was taking control since she said she would when she handcuffed him to the bed. She unzipped him and cupped him and began kneading him.

"OMG! You are killing me!"

"Just hold on … I want it at its best!" She rubbed it a few more times and said, "That is perfect for me. Hold my leg," she threw her right leg across his left arm. She held on to his neck and stared into his eyes. "Now go slowly." He did and his knees buckled. He put both his hands on her buttocks and brought her all the way in and his extension was vibrating, and she was already in the zone. Biting her lip, she said, "Give it to me," and she arched which made her tighter.

He did and then in the middle was paradise. That's the spot she likes. She was squealing and trying not to scream. "So so good Beatrice I can't wait any longer." "Don't wait...I am on my second," and he did. She was kissing him and sucking on his tongue. He like her to kiss hard when he was driving for the touchdown. The best for him. He knew she liked him kissing on her breast while in the motion.

They were perfect in every way. She stood and licked his lips. Putting their foreheads together and looking into each others eyes. He was holding her waist and she was holding his shoulders. "You want to try again it will be awhile before we get this chance again?"

She turned around and touched the floor long red hair falling around her face, and he looked her her beautiful derriere.

"This is the way I remember we did it the first time … oh no … you are wiggling oh sh.... Don't you dare … stop!" He had her hips firmly.

It was as intense and as fast as the first time and he was gone to the moon.

CHAPTER THREE

Roscoe and Beatrice walked back into the party, just as prim and proper as before. She had freshened up in the downstairs bathroom and had found her stored perfume bottle behind the towels where she had put it days ago. "Good thinking," she said to herself. She patted her thong with a dose of Jasmine. Kyleigh likes this perfume, too.

As pre- teens they had been called "the Jassy twins."

Some people never change. Beatrice and Kyleigh prided themselves on not changing the good stuff.

"Dance with me Roscoe by the pool," he walked with her admiring her height. No one had ever made him feel like she did. He was her king and now was the time to enjoy each other. They had danced the night away at Guy and Kyleigh's wedding. Now he was holding her just the way he did then.

Except he was eating the Jasmine off her neck, and it was doing a number on her.

"Roscoe I think something is wrong with me?"

"What my love?" he looked concerned.

"I want you again. Do you think this is normal? I maybe a nymphomaniac," softly she said it.

"No you are making up for the times we can't. That's

normal. We may overcompensate, but if we both enjoy. It is the best. Most people would die for what we have. In the future people will say that's a nice old couple. They don't need to know, we jump each others' bones every chance we get. Now stop your worrying. OK?"

"OK ... Let's go back into this grand party."

Kyleigh met them. "You two look worn out!"

"Can give no info … or I have to kill you," Beatrice said.

"Where is Madeline?" BeBe wanted to know.

"Over there with her friends," pointing to where Madeline and a small black lady stood.

Jackie couldn't believe her eyes, "GM you clean up nicely. Who's been fixing your hair? I love the red dress and heels on you. You never told me you are rich. All these years you been wearing that ponytail and them cowboy boots had me fooled."

Jackie was talking a mile a minute.

"Don't you 'all give her anymore Champagne she may spill all my secrets!"

"The first answer is at Blaine's in Dallas. They do my hair, but surprise ... we are moving back. Just so you can do my hair."

"Really?Just for me! I am so happy I could cry!"Jackie said.

"Yep! Now the champagne has got her crying!" GM smiled.

She had dressed up for GM in a leopardskin fitted midi and wore black platform heels. Her hair was piled with a hair weave laced with gold to accentuate the large gold hoops dangling from her ears. Madeline knew she was trying to impress her friends and she was doing a good job. She would have plenty to brag about at that beauty shop tomorrow!

"Can I hug you GM?"Jackie asked.

"Sure you can. I am so glad you came. I have a reason for you to be here. Trevor come here." Over walks a six foot four handsome man and puts his arm around Madeline's waist.

Jackie says, "I hope you know him and does he have a wife?" She was looking from side to side, looking for a fight to start.

"Yes, Miss Jackie I have a wife," Trevor said.

"Where is she? You had better get your hands off GM. Her son will shoot you. He's a cop you know!" she was hyperventilating.

"Now now Miss Jackie. Madeline IS my wife," Trevor laughed.

"I don't know no Madeline," shaking her head.

This tall man said, "Yes you do here she is … your GM is my Madeline and we are very married. Tell her darling," kissing her on the cheek.

"Jackie, he is my Prince Charming and we are married and living in the great state of Texas right now!"

She almost fainted. Guy had to help her to a chair.

"I just wanted to see how strong you was," she didn't want anyone to think she was weak.

"I am so glad you are sitting down. I have made arrangement to build you a beauty shop of your very own. I will talk details about it later when we get completely moved back. Sound good?"

"She has fainted. Get the ammonia. There is a doctor here. Jackie! Jackie! She is out. Trev can you lie her on the couch. I'll get a wet washcloth!"

Trevor toted the five foot black woman to the couch and laid her down.

"Light as a feather. Madeline you got to feed this woman," Trevor quipped.

"Jackie ... he wants you to cook him a home cooked meal. So wake yourself up."

She opened one eye … "Do I have to? I was enjoying the ride," Jackie was grinning.

"You play with my man again and you won't be getting that beauty shop!"

And they all burst out laughing.

Madeline said, "I have missed my dear friend."

"And I have missed that mouth of yours most," Jackie said. "Just the way you say ... Don't forget to get your tip my miracle worker."

"Trev Trevor! Did she tell you I can perform miracles? That's the best stuff I have never EVER drank. Did make me a little woozy ..."

She got up and swayed those hips all the way to the coffeepot and said, "Can one of you ... strong man pour me a cup of coffee?" turning to wink at Madeline who was killing herself laughing.

"Trev didn't I tell you she was a character?" GM stated.

She sipped her champagne and looked into Trevor's eyes,

"I don't know what I would have done after Breast Cancer without her. I was taking radiation treatments and really down. She made me laugh all through that time and she keep my spirits up. That's why I love her."

"I do understand … so go easy on that. I can pick you up but I've got a bad back," he was rubbing his right flank as if it hurt.

"Since when? If that's the case with that bad back we can't ..." she whispered the rest.

"My back is fine. I think I will carry your long legs up that staircase right now!"

"Not now I have to see to my other guests," and she did a Jackie on him, and swayed her hips so that the slit of her red dress, was showing a lot of leg and her heels were clicking his tune.

He sheepishly was looking from side to side to see if anyone else was watching.

"I got to go to speak to Sophie Trev. Do you want to come?"

"No, I'll pass," and walked over to see Guy.

Sophie was popping that chewing gum that she loved so well.

"Sophie darling, you look so cute! I am so glad you could come." Sophie had on a blue and white polka dot fitted dress on that was cut low low in the front.

"Must show off the girls," Sophie ran her finger down her cleavage. Her hair was in a beehive as usual. She had on red shoes and a red pocketbook. She was trying to spruce up and be sophisticated.

"And who might you be?" Sophie asked.

"It's me GM . Just got a little dressed up for my grandson's party. You remember him, don't you?"

"Yes … he is the one that likes the boobies. He rides a motorbike. I remember. Did he marry a girl with bigguns?"

"There they are ... see the happy couple over there! What do you think Sophie?"

"I think he got cheated. She's as flat as a pancake. But he does look at no one else ... so it might work!" closing one eye and tilting her head sideways, as she did when a customer was trying to cheat her out of a tip.

"Sophie I brought you here to tell you something," Madeline smiled at Sophie.

"Well tell me I am dying to know. It isn't bad is it?" frowning.

"No silly woman," slapping her on her hand as they did when they were young.

"Then open that trap of yours and tell me," Sophie pouted.

"I am going to build you ... your own cafe. What do you think about that?"

Sophie stood with her hands on her hips and a red pocketbook dangling from one of them, like she was not impressed.

"I don't know nothing about running no cafe ... We went to school together. You know ... I didn't to well in math and business stuff! IT gives me the hives. I thank you though."

"What if you had a manager and a secretary to do the bookwork? And all you had to do was cook and serve … or hire a cook and serve as you do now?"

"How much does it pay?" Sophie asked.

"You will make all the profits and eventually can sit back and make money off the name on the building." Madeline paused, seeing Sophie's wheels turning slowly.

"What you think of that?"she asked her friend.

"I think if you run it. GM I will work for you!" She still had not gasped what GM was saying.

"We will talk about it later," she gave up for now.

"In school you was always the bright one, GM. I was lucky to have you as my friend!" she almost teared up.

"Get yourself some more champagne and something to eat,"

Madeline quickly said before she ruined her own makeup.

"There ain't nothing to eat here … well nothing to stick to your ribs. I wish that tall white haired man would come over here. I'd like to stick to his ribs." Sophie was cackling and patting her purse that she had brought up to her chest to hold.

Madeline put her hands on her hips and squared off in front of Sophie. "That's my husband you are talking about!"

"I knew that, I was just having some fun with you, GM. Like we use to in the good old days!" Sophie winked.

"Yep we did have some good times. So YOU want a rib joint instead of a cafe. Does that sound better than a cafe?"

"Absolut-n -tooting! It sounds better. I am a happy woman. I am going to get me some meat on my bones. I drank too many of those green bottles of beer with a H……… I'll see you later honey. Got to go … hug hug! kiss kiss!" and she was out the door.

"Trevor help me find Lefty," Madeline was getting tired, it had been a long flight and jet lag was getting to her.

He pointed to a group of men in the corner, there was Lefty. She and Trevor walked over to him. She said, "Lefty can I speak to you for just a minute?"

He followed her into the kitchen, "It seem to be quieter in there. Do you remember me?"

"I remember a woman with a ponytail wearing cowboy boots that kinda looked like you!" Lefty said.

Standing there in her Louis Vuitton heels that were killing her feet, "I wish I had my cowboy boots on now!" and laughed.

"You probably know my grandson better?" Roscoe came around the corner.

"Hey, man. How's it going?"

He shook Trevor's hand and then Roscoe's.

"Because of you good people, I am a foreman now and working with some real good people. They promoted Frank to superintendent and he promoted me up. The best thing that has happened is Adam is in jail and his cousin. Hopefully for along time!"

"Can't thank you enough ... Sir can I have your permission to hug her neck?"

"Sure as long as it is a one time deal," Trevor said.

Madeline hugged him and patted him on the back like one of the guys.

Trevor was grinning at Madeline. A look she knew well. Pat him again and I am coming after you woman …

The party was weaning and the well wishers were leaving. The mayor welcomed Trevor after he heard a "Trevor Alexander Porter" was going to build down by the lake.

This was a big deal for the town.

Trevor had signed papers when he got here today.

Madeline and Trevor were home were home and she had decided to help Jana. She was pacing with two dogs following her every step.

Trevor was standing on the second floor balcony watching her. "What on earth is going on in that pretty little head of yours?" he asked himself. He was going to find out tonight.

She was talking to someone on her cell phone, "Yes I will help. Now tell me what can I do?"

He saw her listening to the person on the phone.

"I have been through this before and it is hard not to have flashbacks. I thought it was all dead and buried."

Then she turned saw Trevor and she paled, and continued talking.

"I am going to talk to my husband and see if he has any ideas. Be safe. We will talk tomorrow," Madeline hung up.

"Now what have you got yourself into? No more PI work. We agreed."

"Yes we did, but this is for Jana!" Madeline declared.

"She okay? Is she still in Japan?" he needed to just listen but he was so worried about his wife. He knew her well. She had just committed herself to doing something dangerous. He could feel it in his bones.

She came to see me last week and asked for my help. I did not give her an answer until now. I will fill you in. Then you and tell me what to do or what we can do?"

She poured them both a brandy. They sat on the glider looking at the starry sky. He still had said nothing.

"I now have you to help me. Way back then, all I wanted to do was run. If we are moving back to North Carolina eventually, I want to clear this up who killed Sam while we are here in Dallas. Can you understand?"

"I agreed ...YOU need closure," swirling his brandy and he took a large drink of his finest.

"That girl is desperate as I would be to help her husband. My son is undercover! I have to say it again and again. I have misjudged him all these years. I have hated him. I was told by that SHERIFF Thomas that Bruce was in on it. I was in shock. I had blinders on. What do you think should be our first move?" patting his thigh.

"If this sheriff has ties to this Japanese drug smuggling outfit. It is going to be dangerous. I don't want you involved. I will look into it," he chugged his brandy because the fireworks were about to begin.

She was furious. She had run GM & GS Private Investigation Service for many a year. "So you are saying you can play, but I can't? I do have experience in this kind of work and I thought we were partners in everything?"

"I know you do honey," she saw this tall hunk of a man turn away... "I just don't want to lose you ..."

"OH Trev! You are not going to lose me... I am stuck

like glue on you. We are one now," she put her arm in his and stared at the moon.

"Sam was my friend, too and I did not pursue any killer, but Shackleford. I feel guilty for that, but I will get this sheriff but you leave it to me. Is that clear? What about Jana?"

"She is adamant that Bruce can be cleared. If we help her. I have to help her. She has poured her heart out to me about how much she loves my Bruce. I think it is high time I see my son."

"I agree we will go see him. We are a team on everything. Didn't you say that?" he took her hand gently and kissed it while gazing into her eyes.

"OK I have work to do and calls to make for the business. Can you locate where this sheriff is working? That is a starting point. I need to see Jana to see where she is in her investigation so we do not duplicate."

"Ask her to come here so we can put our heads together," Trevor made that clear.

Madeline was thinking and said it out loud, "I am so glad Guy is not here!"

"Me, too! Honey, me too! Now let's get some sleep," Trevor escorted her to their bedroom.

They showered together like two teenagers in the huge shower. He told her he was never too tire to make love to her.

Sheriff Thomas was still working at the sheriff department, but he was not as sheriff. Trevor would just test the waters a bit, asking too many questions could raise a red flag. He wanted to find out why this man was demoted.

Madeline was on her way to work and the limo dropped her off at the front door when a man approached her, "I hear you are looking for a buyer? I want to give you my card." Her bodyguards were there immediately, but made no scene just waiting for her signal of distress.

The man turned and disappeared into the horde of people. She thought that strange, but tucked the card in her business suit pocket. It was something she would investigate later.

For now GM & GS Oil Refineries was her and her grandson's baby. Business was as usual and the steady paperwork kept her busy all morning. She had talked to Guy by Skype and business matters had been discussed this way for sometime.

Trevor showed up for lunch and they ate. He asked her if she had contacted Jana yet? Do and bring her home tonight with you. No reason to prolong this matter," as he was eating the salad she had ordered for him.

"You know I can't stand these things," Trevor was looking at his fork and grimaced as if it was disgusting.

"I know you can't. I have to take care of my big man now. Don't I?" she was batting her eyelashes at him.

"Okay you win this one," kissing her hand because that is all she allowed him to kiss in public.

Madeline picked Jana up on her way home. Jana remembered seeing the white limo when working for Jared, but had never ridden inside it. It was the world her Bruce had been born into, and he had left it all behind to go to Japan. She was in deep thought about their romance when Madeline spoke.

"Are you okay, my dear?" she asked Jana.

"Yes. I'm fine. I am looking forward to meeting your husband. You said he is in on clearing Bruce's name."

"I said he will help us arrest Sheriff Thomas for the murder of my Sam. They were friends," Madeline looked out the window as they drove by the long white fence up to the mansion. She was suddenly consumed by grief and began to sob. Jana handed her a Kleenex and hugged her mother-in-law.

Madeline had held that in for so long ... so long! She let no one in her family see her cry. She had to be strong for them way back then.

Jana understood the grieving process well. She had grieved the lost of Bruce. She had been celebrating this week of their reuniting.

"Let it out. I have cried for Bruce for so long ... so long. It was like a death. A death of our marriage," Jana said.

"I have not adjusted to thinking of Bruce not being in cahoots with Sheriff Thomas. It pointed to them. I tried to get Bruce to tell me, I was wrong. He only said, "Think what you will mother. He left, as if guilty."

Jana said, "He told me when we were first married that he was sad that his father had been killed. That his wife was dead and his mother hated him. My son is with her, my little GUY. He has never said anything to me since about it. No matter how much I probed."

"We will go in and talk with Trevor," Madeline had reapplied her makeup in the car. There was no traces of her tears as they entered the house.

Trevor was waiting and they discussed everything and came up with a plan. Each one knew what the other one had to do. Trevor had contacts in Dallas, but this one was for Jim. Jim was a police officer and working on another case. So nothing would be unusual about him being at the

Dallas Police Department. He had excess to files that they needed. He always thought of Trevor as his older brother. Their families were that close.

Jana had only one contact that she trusted and her name was Rosie. Rosie was an expert in technically demanding research. She was asked to trace all the calls the sheriff made and record them. Their phone numbers could lead to this Mao Jung. They needed to collect all the evidence. Proof of a connection between these two would be crucial, if they were to be prosecuted.

Jana was assigned security guards to protect her. Trevor had hugged her and told her she was now in their family. She was asked to stay with them.

They had twenty bedrooms. "We have plenty of room for you. The bodyguards will take you to get your clothes from the hotel tonight or tomorrow your call, hon!"

"I'll just go in with you tomorrow and I feel better in the light of day. People know me at GM & GS Oil. So I will not come in, but you can call me when you are ready to come home and we can move my things then." She leaned and hugged her mother-in-law.

Madeline got out of the limo and into work as usual.

Trevor made some calls to some of his past colleagues that they owed him a favor. Bernie was a prison warden in another state. He will have access to how to get Bruce out without much hoopla.

Jana had convinced them.Bruce was telling them the truth.

Trevor knew Bruce's mother would fight for him. It was going to have to go through the court so he needed a judge. He lived in Dallas and he knew them all. He was going to call in a favor from his uncle, who was a judge. He could be on alert, and in the future arrange to be on the bench, when Bruce was brought there.

He had told Madeline, "Darling just focus on the business. Then all will look normal. Jana and I, and an army of my friends will be working on this."

She was a hard-headed woman so he was going to watch her close. He may have to eat CRAP salad every day.

The months were flying by and Kyleigh was decorating the nursery finally. Her November ultrasound showed them, they were going to have a boy! Guy had squeezed her hand and she could see his chest expanding while the obstetrician was explaining the findings.

She had called Beatrice and now that she was not regurgitating all over the place, they could get her nursery done.

Beatrice would find out next month what her twins were going to be. She would help Kyleigh. "That's what friends are for, but don't expect me to tote anything."

"We can get matching umbrella strollers and put them in our cars. Then we will have something to put our goodies in …"

"What are you talking about B?" Kyleigh said looking at her to explain.

"Well K! I cannot carry myself around let alone a bunch of packages. Haven't you noticed I am twice as big as you?"

"B you have always been twice as big as me!" "You do have a point. James will go everywhere we want to go, Poor Man! He has no clue what he is in for," holding their fat little tummies and laughing.

They went to every Baby shop they could find. Only after scouring the internet for the right piece.

Beatrice said, "Why don't you let them deliver?"

"I will I just want to see it first. Sometimes, it is entirely different when you get it home. Besides we two would never get out of the house without the brothers with us."

"You are right Kyleigh. The curtains have been decided? Momma said she would be honored, if you would let her sew them and papa said papa said he would hang them as your baby shower gift."

"That is so sweet! Today we shall look for that fabric. Take the swatch with us to the other shops," Kyleigh almost jumped with excitement.

"I will draw a sketch and we can place it on the sketch pad to see whether anything we see will clash. Have you thought about that navy blue crib and chest of drawers?"

"Yes that will be perfect and something we don't have to go and eyeball. I'll have it delivered tomorrow. Isn't this fun?"

"It would be more fun, if I didn't have to pee every five minutes!" They both laughed. James was at the car and bodyguards were with them in every store. They went and carried packages as needed.

"Kyleigh it is nice to have an extra set of hands to help us," as the men loaded the packages in the car.

"Yes fellows, be glad the heavy stuff is being delivered."

"Thank you ma'am," and he went back to his post.

"Guy insisted they be with us at all times, and he will let the furniture people in since he works from home. He wants no one in that house unless he is there."

"Roscoe, too! You'd think they were brothers!"

They stopped at an ice cream parlor on the way home.

They were having cravings. They told their husbands over the phone. "Yum so good so good!"

Guy said, "Stop that right now!"

Roscoe said, "Stop that right now!"

The girls hung up and in unison said, "Yep they are brothers!" giggling so all the patrons could hear.

"These people are clueless. Yum so gooood!"

"I'll see you tomorrow, BeBe!" as they dropped her off and drove next door to the top of the hill.

Where Guy ws standing at the back door, that is where she always came to take the elevator since she had gained weight.

He took her in his arms and said, "Don't ever do that in public," kissing her neck.

"What on earth are you talking about my dear husband of mine?" batting her eyelashes at him.

"Yum yum so good is for my ears only!"

"It was ice cream honey! Ice cream ...oh yes! I see what you mean." Guy had her in the downstairs bathroom by then, and she promised herself to go shopping more, and bring home ice cream every time.

"Beatrice what kind of stunt was that!" Roscoe said. "I nearly wrecked the truck." "I was JUST eating ice cream. What is wrong with you? Keep on right there YesYesYes!"

The court was quiet and Bruce was in his seat. Trevor, Madeline, and Jana were behind him. He was in the handsomest black tailored suit that Jana could find, He was clean shaven and his hair was long but clean.

He said to himself, "Don't get your hopes up fool!" but when Jana told him his mother was helping to get him out … his heart caved in … and he would dare to hope.

The court came into session and they all rose. Judge Ernest J. Porter presiding … it was a long discussion and he was granted bail and to be under the supervision by his mother Madeline Smith, at all times. They did not use her married name of Porter. Both names were legal since she used one for business. Their lawyer was pleading for a retrial stating that all the facts had not been presented at the last court appearance.

Trevor's uncle stared at him when he hit the gavel and said, "Granted!"

They rode home to the ranch. No one said a word.

James was driving through the traffic especially careful because he knew this was a big deal. He had never picked someone in the family up from court.

A prisoner … that he knew as a young boy. Bruce and he had played together. James's mother, Estelle had been Mr. Samuel Smith's cook and Mrs. Madeline's confidante. Since she had passed Mrs. Madeline had kept the twin boys on parole for the last ten years. That was in the papers she had signed, relinquishing the business.

James and John were more than chauffeurs. They were like family and would do anything for Mrs. Madeline.

Bruce shook James's hand when he got out. Trevor patted Bruce on the back, and Bruce shook his hand, also.

Madeline and Jana had gone on in together talking.

Bruce was emotional seeing his mother and wife walking into this house. He had never fathomed this day. He had remembered Trevor slightly ... but never knew how rich he was until now.

Of course, everything would look huge, after being in a tiny cell for so long. He had to talk to Trevor about Unitus, and they did. Trevor said Jana informed him about Unitus.

My friend Bernie at another prison, is the warden. He is going to have him transferred to his prison since he is an undercover government agent. The release would go unnoticed. Unitus will be brought to Southfork to guard the women.

"You do agree these women need guarding?" They both laughed.

"I can't tell you how humble I am right now! I will forever be indebted to you," he paused and walked to look skyward.

"Jana said you could do miracles, but I am not a person who believes in miracles ...UNTIL today. Thank you Trevor!" and he hugged him as he would his own father.

He was hugging him as Madeline yelled, "You two come and eat!"

She had not spoken to Bruce in ten years so she avoided it at the kitchen table. The chef had fixed a feast for his home-coming. He could not eat much. He was not use to it. He had a hunger for something other than food and he was staring at Jana.

She was avoiding his stare and talking to Madeline as if they had been friends all of their lives. These two are going to be the death of Trevor and me.

He thought his mother would talk to him, but now he realized she didn't know what to say. She was the one that turned him away.

He still had a bitter taste in his mouth. She still loves me or she would not have helped Jana. My Jana is amazing. She cannot look at me without wrapping herself around me.

That is a good reason … we must be civilized.

"Would you like some brandy, Bruce?"

"That sounds great my friend!"

The men retired to the den and were laughing an hour later when the women said their good-nights."

Bruce was raising to leave and follow, Trevor said. "Sit down my boy! They will be chattering for another thirty minutes and then they will be primping for another thirty minutes. In one hour you had better get out of my way!"

Bruce entered their room and went straight for the shower. He showered and there she sat in a bubble bath. He had thought she was in the bed. The bathroom light were off and it was so large, the shower and Jacuzzi tub was on opposite side of the double marble vanity.

He saw her in the moonlight that shone down from the

skylight. She rose to extended her arms for him to come to her. He had not dried off fully and he was having trouble breathing as he always did when he came near her.

"Come to me my husband … I need you so!"

He was in her so fast he had to stop himself. He went slow the way she liked it. She expanded her small body that was accommodating him. Minute by minute he was swelling more and more.

He was thinking of everything but her. To block his mind to hold his love in check … until she was ready and she would beg, "Please honey now! Bruce now!"

Those were the sweet words on this earth and the words he long to hear every night. He could not ignore those words … and she knew it … any willpower he had was gone.

He lay on his back still attached and he said to her … "You are in control tonight. You love me like you want to!" Just giving her free reign had increased her needs. He was hitting her G-spot. They were doubling up with pleasure untold.

"Sheriff Thomas so good to see you!" said Madeline.

"I'm not sheriff anymore and you know it," she gave him her puzzled face. "What are you talking about?" She had her wire in her bra so she had to get closer.

"Your family ruined me, but I got your husband back. Don't play that innocent female thing with me. You knew I had the hots for you and I made sure that husband of yours would not be around."

She told herself to stay calm and talk sweet things to him. NO that is something she would never do, not even for evidence. "OH really? Tell me more big guy?"

He was biting. "You could have never hurt my husband.

He would have beat you to a pulp!" She had to bait more, men like him did not want a woman to have the upper hand or the last word. She knew the bodyguards were near. If she gave the signal, they would be there in a sec.

"Not from his grave, honey. I put him there!"

She lost it. She was fixing to hit him so hard, but her bodyguard came up and said, "You have a call on your cell phone, Miss Madeline!" She walked off.

He was a good man. Pete saw her face and sensed she was going to erupt. He was Roscoe's friend and he had seen her go off on Roscoe before. It had scared him so bad as a little boy that he had never forgotten that face.

His intervention had probably saved the recording. If she had started hitting the sheriff, she could not have stopped.

More than a tape would have gotten damaged!

"Here's another piece of evidence!" Handing it to Trevor and did not look left or right. He was going to blow the roof off. Before that happened, she marched herself to the bar and fixed herself a martini. It had been a hard day at the office and elsewhere.

Bruce hear a roar of a lion in the den, "What in the hell were you thinking? He could have killed you!"

He walked around the table and put some distance between them.

She said, "Pete was with me every step of the way. He just didn't know where I was going or who I was going to talk to!"

Bruce walked in, "Is everything all right?"

Trevor was fuming, "You need to talk some sense into your mother. Listen to this!" he played the recording and Bruce went pale.

"I would never want you to put yourself in danger for me, mother ... I can fight my own battles and have for a very long time. Trevor is right! You were in danger today... real danger!

"You two amaze me. Remember, I did this for a living for ten years! No one has bossed me around like you two, and lived to tell about it!" she stomped to her room.

Jana said to Trevor and Bruce, "I see where Bruce got his temper from!"

Trevor said, "Yes his father was the opposite! A soft spoken man that love her feisty, as I do!"

"Beatrice we have all the things for our nursery. Can you give your momma a call?" Kyleigh was sitting in her lime green rocker - glider.

She was exhausted and her feet were swollen.

"Of course, I can my little slave driver! Just remember I will be finding out next week what we need for decorating MY nursery. You, my friend will be pounding the pavement to help me!" and she winked as she dialed her mother's number.

Kyleigh curled one side of her lip like Elvis used to do, and continued rubbing her feet.

The curtains were matched to the navy and lime and a magical plaid was chosen. Her nursery was going to be bright. The walls have been painted a "Carolina Blue."

She and Guy had found a teak rocking horse to last for generations. The wall decorations Guy had picked out. His favorite football, baseball, basketball and hockey figurines would be displayed on a teak bookshelf along with a variety of children's books.

Kyleigh had loved books so her mother had gone

through their library in the Middleton's home and gave Kyleigh everyone she had asked for. She could start reading to her angel, now.

Beatrice's mom and dad had done a fabulous job on the window treatments. They would take no money, it was a gift.

CHAPTER SIX

Tate's grades were good, B's and one A-plus which was in art. No one knew he like to draw not even Adam. Chris Shackleford his uncle … I mean his father, was not in his childhood. He recalled he only sent money to Adam saying, "Your uncle is thinking about you!" That was only once a year. So his father only thought of him, once a year.

Aunt Eunice hugged him and told him how proud she was of him. The brats came and hugged him, too! He had to admit that was pretty neat.

He had to thank Jennifer for helping him. After Christmas, she would be on her way to college. She was a smart girl and had a full scholarship to Duke for four years. She told him if he kept his grades up he could get a scholarship. Maybe not to Duke, but another college. He was going to try.

The thirteen year old skateboarder, Corey and he had bonded and they every afternoon flew down the empty sidewalks to the school parking lot. There they practiced maneuvers and it was another outlet to keep him out of trouble.

He had not missed that old gang, they were no good.

They hurt people every chance they got. He had never done that, but it was on their next step for him. He had to, or he would be out of the gang.

There was the cutest Blonde girl sitting at their dinner table. She was a friend of hippie- dippie Coraine. She had started making eyes at him.

"Oh no! This was going to be a test!" He told himself. The girls had been all over him, but none here at this school. This was the first one, and his hormones were high gear. He had to be excused from the table and he went into his room. Now he had a real bed in the boys' bunk bed room. He had rolled the air mattress up and stowed it under the new bed. He was lost in his art when in walks this girl ... half naked.

The boys were asleep. She was supposedly spending the night with Coraine, who was past out. This would be nice but he was not going to do anything to get kicked out of this house. He told her to leave ... he was not interested. She came closer and rubbed herself against him. He did not move and said … "get out girlie!"

She was asking for it … no way … he walked her out.

She said, "Don't ever forget my name is Debbie and I will pay you back for this one day!" She took her cute little ass to Coraine's room and probably masturbated herself to sleep. He knew, he sure did.

The next morning, he finished drawing her picture. It was stamped in his brain. Every little detail magnified. He was focusing on "This is what will get you behind bars, if she is below eighteen!" Adam had said, "Don't mess with this. Only mess with older women!"

Beatrice had her ultrasound and Roscoe was holding

her hand when they were told they were having twin boys. She smiled up at him.

"Two boys … Are you sure?" Roscoe asked the doctor.

He pointed to the two male genitals. Roscoe nodded and a big grin came across his face which made Beatrice so happy.

"You my love, give me everything!" Roscoe was kissing her all over. Immediately the doctor left the room. "Everything I have ask for. You have given me, my boys! Yes Yes! You are the man!" she shook her head up and down.

"Go buy the cigars and I will get home the best way I can," and she put on her sad face.

"Oh no you don't … You know we will celebrate this tonight! Capeesh?"

Then she smiled. She knew how they were going to celebrate!

The next day she called Kyleigh and told her ...boys!

"I know Roscoe told Guy last night!"

"You got to be kidding, the snake! He was busy all night!"

"I know Roscoe told him that, too!"

"I guess you want me to help you shop for that nursery of yours?" Kyleigh teased.

"Why yes! I believe I do … so come on over!"

"Kyleigh arrived, and Beatrice was still in sweatpants,

"Aren't we going shopped?" Kyleigh asked.

"Of course, we are! Whatever gave you the idea we weren't?" Beatrice asked.

"Well for one, you aren't dressed to go shopping!"

"I most certainly am," Beatrice glared at her … like I dare you to question my attire.

"Sweats are perfect for shopping online. While we were shopping for you, I had my sketch pad remember?"

"Yes I do remember you took a lot of notes," Kyleigh said. "OMG... you are so smart!"

"Did you think I was going to walk all over those stores again? When my feet were killing me. I was trying to look so sophisticated. Now all I have to do is, click click and it is done!" Beatrice sighed.

"I knew it was going to be boys … Two little mama's boys," and they squealed.

Everything was delivered the next day and the nursery was set up all except the curtains which her momma and papa were making as of yesterday. She had faxed her mother a picture of the swatch. She had pick a swatch for either a girl or boy's room ... same with the furniture. So life was simple. Roscoe's eyes were aglow when he got home he asked, "How did you do this, Bebe?"

"I have magical powers."

"I know you do and we are going to use those powers all the way to the delivery room. Aren't we, my love?"

"You betcha," and it was onto the celebrating!

The curtains were hung in two days in the boys nursery. They were navy & hunter green, and white & yellow plaid. There was two of everything. The walls remained white. The two cribs were hunter green and the comforters were baby blue with a yellow thread running through the pale green which matched Beatrice's eyes. The two glider chairs matched her pale green eyes, also.

Roscoe could help her pick out the wall stuff after Christmas. It was too close to the holidays to shop except for Christmas presents.

This was their first Christmas in the new house. Who would have thought this would have happened when they met at Guy and Kyleigh's wedding?

Beatrice told Kyleigh, "I could have never dreamed this!"

Kyleigh replied, "Not in a hundred years!"

They hugged and rubbed their tummies as the babies were kicking. They rocked and looked out at the mountains and down at the lake. Just chatting, when in came Jana and Madeline.

"What a beautiful sight! My two girls are looking good!"

Madeline said.

Jana said, "Next year three little boys will be running after granny next Christmas! So you two ... relax and enjoy this!"

"You are right granny. You will be busy next year because I will be GREAT nana and all they do is sit in the rocking chair and rock!" Madeline said.

Jana put her hand over her mouth and said, "OMG … You are right! I will be a granny. I must call my mother," and she paused.

"She wants to come and see her Brucie this Christmas. I was hoping everything would be settled," Jana said.

"Don't worry, hon. They will be welcome at the ranch. It is almost finished around the corner. WE had twenty bedrooms in Dallas and we will have twenty here. They can come this year. That's why Trevor and I brought you and Bruce here. We want you to stay with us. Unless you want to move to Japan, after he is cleared. You talk about it. I guarantee Trevor is talking to him about it now."

Jana said, "He is waiting for Guy to open up to him. I know it is hard. I am giving him his space for his decision. Bruce will not make one till he is clear. He is a proud man."

"Yes, he is like his father. He is a very wise man.. he picked you for his wife!" Madeline said.

The girls chimed in their agreement.

The security was still tight and Roscoe was doing a great job to keep the family safe especially through the holidays.

"It can be a rough time in my line of business," he told Beatrice.

"I know honey, you are my hero … Now tell me is Santa coming down our chimney this year?" batting her eyelashes.

"Yes, I guess you want me to clean the chimney, too!"

"You betcha big guy! The builders may have overlooked that tedious chore before we light a fire in it!"

"I will see to it Beatrice! Don't bother Roscoe! He is so busy!" Madeline said. Kyleigh was poking her and smiling.

Then she whispered, "GM that is not what she wants him to do!" and winked at her.

Beatrice's eyes had not left Roscoe's so she had not seen Kyleigh informing Madeline about their cleaning habits.

Madeline was shocked and said, "This new generation."

She blew a kiss to Guy and slapped the back of her neck.

Kyleigh said plopping a Christmas mint in her mouth, "Guy has to learn to wash dishes!"

Madeline's reaction was priceless, "Trevor! Oh Trevor dear I need you to help me … wrap some presents tonight!"

He nodded.

"That wasn't a good one, Kyleigh. We have servants that do everything for us. Yes we are out of the loop! We are so old fashion anyways. Watch this!" Madeline continued.

"Trevor honey … you don't have to do manual labor. You have better things to do!" batting her eyelashes.

"Madeline he sure is in a hurry to get your coat! Uh huh!"

They flew back to Dallas and were still working on Bruce's case. It was looking good. They had hired a new female attorney named Adriana, and she was handling the paperwork and judges with kid gloves. She may just pull it off.

The more she delved in the case, the more the ex- sheriff squirmed. She told Madeline she was going to nail him to the wall.

"Not only is the creep that contracted a hit to kill a man but my sources say he is running a human- trafficking ring. I need you to ask Bruce when you get home, if he knows anything about it. If I call your house, it maybe traced. So talk in a safe place. Trevor has advised me you 'all have one. Call me and have a happy holiday!"

Bruce told her that,"Sheriff Thomas was connected to Mao Jung for cocaine that was a fact, but anything else he had no knowledge of. This woman has too much on her plate. You and she talk best, ask her to focus on my case separate from that. If she pushes to hard with Jung, he will have her wasted THAT is a fact! And I will be back to square one, and no lawyer. Jung would not be upset, if the sheriff was incarcerated because he is a peon. Explain as only you can that her life would be in jeopardy, and that mine would be over, too!" she kissed him on the cheek.

"OK son ... I know you would be killed, too! We will not have that! It has taken me too long to see the light!"

CHAPTER SEVEN

The Christmas party was at Trevor and Madeline's new house down by the lake. Only family was invited. It was so good to be home. It was so good to have Bruce and Guy reunited. Her grandson had always loved his dad. He just took my view and she felt guilty for a lot of things. Bruce told her not to... "because if you have not left with Guy and signed those papers, they would have killed the both of you. Jared Banks and his conies were pieces of trash. He was clenching his fists and gritting his teeth and pacing.

Trevor came in, "Jana wants you to help her Bruce." Bruce calmed and walked out to find his Jana.

"I had to say something, honey. Now tell me what has him all worked up?"

"He has forgiven me, but not Banks. The man is dead. He has too much anger, he can not get on the stand. Adriana is a flake, but has won and won her cases. I will tell you all Bruce has said about her. I am just having my doubts right now. We will put all this aside until Christmas is over. Darling, fix me a martini you do it so well!"

She walked to the bar where he was standing and said, "You do everything so well!"

Quickly turning, "I'll be right back." To the powder room to reapply his favorite perfume and place his gift between her breasts. He could not miss it and she smiled.

Guy was standing by Kyleigh rubbing his kicking baby.

"He is going to be a soccer player. A real Davis Beckham! The way he kicks," she nodded her head and rolled her eyes at Guy.

"At lest you don't have... but one ...in there kicking! Roscoe come rub the TWINS." Roscoe went over to his giraffe of a wife and began rubbing her breasts. She smacked his hand.

"What did I do? She asked and I delivered!" They all burst out laughing.

"That will go down in the memory book for sure. She writes down everything. Does Kyleigh?" Roscoe asked.

Guy's face went pale, "God I hope not! If she is, we are in a heap of trouble!"

"What do you mean, Bro?" Roscoe was curious.

"You are just nosy. Tell him Dad," Guy said to Bruce.

Bruce closed his eyes. It was the first time in many years that Guy had called him DAD.

"What were you two talking about?" Bruce asked.

"The wives are writing everything down in a memory book . Is Jana doing that?" Guy filled him in.

"OH Boy! If she is I am in a heap of trouble!" Bruce said.

Roscoe said, "Like father like son ... To say the same thing. What have you 'all been up to, that I haven't?" They all laughed and said it was man code, when the girls came up.

"It's only man talk!" They all chimed in, "For men ONLY!"

Roscoe said to the group, "They will be giving us a time tonight! Mine will be bribing me with her sexy lingerie to tell what we said .... Dang! I can't wait to get home!"

"Whoa Bro … You can't leave! You have to eat," Guy said.

You are right. I am eating for two ... I mean she is … I mean, I have been working a lot lately!" hanging his head down so pitifully.

"Cheer up ... It is Christmas! We will soon have red lingerie floating through the houses like Sugarplums," he gulped.

"I'll see you guys later," they caught him by the shoulders.

"Now Guy you have to eat supper with the family. Get it together."

"You 'all are right. I am only eating one ... I mean eating for one!" Trevor just about howled.

Bruce said, "What in the world has got into these boys?"

Trevor said, "I think Santa brought them champagne early."

Bruce said, "I guess I had better get the same thing, they are drinking!"

Trevor said, "Brandy for me ... Mrs Claus prefers me not drunk on Christmas night!" and looked at the ceiling when he saw Madeline come around the corner.

"Dinner is served. Come and get it!" Madeline called.

Trevor said, "Say that again later!"

Her eyes were saying, "Are you crazy? Not in front of the boys" she didn't say it.

Trevor said, "They are not boys any more. Trust me on that one. They are full grown men, darling. They will soon be fathers so I will start it tonight."

She rolled her eyes and looked down.

Now what have you got there ... and he reached for her gift in her bra. She slapped his hand and said, "Not in front of the MEN!"

They at the table were rolling with laughter. They had no clue what Trevor was reaching for.

The prayer was of thanksgiving and a blessing of this house and the surrounding houses. "The hope and joy of the birth of our new babies in the coming year and this day honoring our Jesus on his birthday!" Trevor was an eloquent speaker.

The food was delicious. The wives had cooked their favorite dishes and put them together so no strangers would serve.

"Family times are special and times to share with only family," that was going to be their motto.

Trevor finally cornered Madeline in a dark space in the den. "Now what have you been hiding? You husband is very jealous of that wrapping paper!"

She let him reach in and she held her head high and placed her long fingers on his hand with the package.

"It is something you have been wanting," smiling lovingly up at him. She could melt him with just a few words.

The boathouse that he had contemplated, was paid for as a Christmas present. She had seen his plans and knew he would not build it until the other Southfork was sold.

"It is my gift and they will be here in January to make your dreams come true," Madeline sighed.

"My dreams have already come true. Thank you my love," Trevor kissed her.

"I guess I will have to buy my own boat," he added.

"Yep and it cannot be a big one," she said.

He stared at her.

"It's a lake, Trevor!"

"Got to share this with the rest. They know I have been in your bra. At least, that it what I was going to do. So hurry and lead the way!"

The men were planning on fishing trips and the women were planning on sitting in rockers on the deck drinking mint juleps.

This was the best . Then the thunder boomed and the lightning struck a tree nearby. It was a downpour that raised the lake. They all stayed by the fire singing carols until the storm had passed........Ending with a silent night!

The men were standing in the den and Trevor said, "I hope this is not an omen. You MEN look out for our house next week."

"We have to fly out tomorrow evening."

Guy said to Madeline as she came in, "Why not Sell?"

"We can talk about it later. I have had an offer. I have not investigated the matter, yet. I would not without you Guy!"

"It is your baby! GM & GS Oil Refineries is yours as far as I am concerned. Trevor and I have to pack up the rest of our things and bring our dogs home, Blackie & Black Magic miss their mommy & daddy," looking at Trevor.

"I know you can handle anything you decide, just take your time to think it through. There is no rush."

"I just hate to see you two flying back and forth so much."

"Don't worry she likes to shop in either state," Trevor said and Madeline swatted him on his arm.

"I think the non alcoholic beverage has done her in. My wife is getting sleepy," Guy said looking into Kyleigh's eyes.

"I think my wife has the same disease. The twins are giving her a fit," Roscoe was looking into Beatrice's eyes.

Jana and Bruce had said good night and went to the same bedroom here as the one in Dallas.

It was the one farthest from Trevor and Madeline's bedroom. No sounds from either couples could be heard. That made them all feel more comfortable.

Bruce was ripping Jana's clothes off her and she was shredding his suit. They were still desperate to make every minute count, encase his trial didn't end in an acquittal.

Jana moaned as they climaxed and he wailed as if in mourning. "I will never be able to live without you again."

He looked into her eyes and said, "I had rather be dead."

She kissed him all over. "You will never have to my husband. I am always with you, to eternity."

Roscoe asked Beatrice as they went into the house, "How are you feeling my love? The boys?"

"Santa had better clean that chimney while he can. I will take a selfie to document by the fireplace how horny we were on Christmas day! All this work you have been doing. She was unbuckling his pants and he was unbuttoning her blouse ... like they were making a tomato sandwich. Teamwork was needed with twins on board.

She got the soft sheepskin rug out of the closet and threw it on the floor, in front of the fireplace, where he had lit a crackling fire. He gently laid her on it and told her how beautiful the mother of his children was.

He was kissing her and she him, and they were adjusting positions like the new book said to do. Until he and she could stand it any longer..... Merry Christmas Yes! Oh Santa Claus you did .... did the chimney proud! It is all cleaned out!

Guy had petite little Kyleigh in his arms and up the steps to the bedroom with the fireplace. He lit it, and the glow was illuminating the room and their lovemaking was mighty toasty!

He was panting, "You want it slow darling?'

"I want more more more!"

"Kyleigh please!"

"I want you to get a speeding ticket ..... faster honey!"

"Okay HOT HOT HOT damn!" Guy said at the top of his lungs.

"Merry Christmas Santa!" Kyleigh said as she sighed.

"Thank you Mrs Claus …. I haven't drove 60 in a 30

IN awhile.... may I tear that ticket up because I can't lose my license to DRIVE!

PART SEVEN

CHAPTER ONE

On the flight home Madeline told Trevor about the man that approached her wanting to buy the company. She said she had his business card in her business suit hanging in the office closet.

"I will research this dude to see if he is legit. If he is ... Guy can come and talk to him with you and me." Trevor made that clear that he didn't trust any smooth talking scam artist with either of them.

"You just want me home canning green tomatoes, don't you?" Madeline was baiting.

"I, prefer red tomatoes, dear. Yes I want you safe with me ... always," rubbing her hand that was in his hand and kissing her cheek.

"Well ... when you put it that way I guess I can handle the position," she batted those eyelashes at him.

They had touchdown at Fort-Worth Airport and John had brought the white limo around to pick them up.

"We need to stop by the office for a minute and then we can go home after that.

"Yes sir!" opening the door for them to get in and stowing their luggage in the trunk.

They walked through the lobby and the employees were saying, "Merry Christmas and Happy New Year!" to them.

Trevor said, "Same to all," and waving.

Madeline was in the elevator and Trevor stepped in, "I guess some woman gave them a nice bonus this year."

"I guess she did. They deserved it. It's been a rough year!"

"Not for me. It has been the best year!" Trevor said.

"Yes dear and you talked the high heels right off me!"

"If we weren't in this elevator..." he suggested.

"You'd do what?" The six foot four grabbed her and put her across one of his shoulders and walked into her office and sat her on her feet, "Any more questions?"

"NO dear, Not a one," Madeline said.

Madeline said, "Let me look for the card before I forget what I came for ..." and he laughed.

She found it right where she remembered she put it. Something had told her to hang on to it. She gave it to Trevor.

"I'll only be a minute. I need to freshen up," she said.

"Do you want me to help you, dear?" he asked.

"No stay where you are ... the staff have enough to gossip about as it is!" Madeline blushed.

"You are right," and he sat at her desk.

She came running out of the bathroom and held her hair brush like a microphone. "Can you say that again louder. I want to record it."

"Record what?" he asked.

"YOU said I was right!" she was smiling.

The card turned out to be legit.

Billionaire Marcus Buchanan wanted to buy GM & GS Oil Refineries and Guy would have to set up the meeting.

Madeline was so happy. She wanted to go home and stay.

Guy and Kyleigh's due date would be soon. So she would run the business until he and Kyleigh could come out.

Their own home, Trevor's Southfork, could not be sold until this Oil business deal went through. Trevor was happy at either place, though the Security out here was not what it was back in Hendersonville.

Guy was so excited about the proposal, and he and Kyleigh were in a battle over what the baby's name should be. Guy thought it should be Samuel "Guy"Steven Smith IV, darling!"

Kyleigh said, "What another one? There are too many. The only one I know, I love. People may get him confused," batting her lashes at him.

"What do you suggest? Ivan after Ivan the Great. We can call him Ivanhoe. Or Madison Kyle Smith and call him Kyle. What do you think?" He had his head in a report and she swatted him with a magazine. That got his attention.

"What was that last name you said?" he asked.

"Madison Kyle Smith," she said.

The more she said it, the more she liked it.

"Madison for Madeline and Kyle for Kyleigh...Madison Kyle Smith will be my first choice."

"That is perfect, sweetums!" kissing her on the cheek.

He still hasn't heard a word.

"Are you listening? This is important!"

"This is too honey ... if I don't get it done ... we may not be able to sell the business. We will soon have to go out to Dallas and finalize it."

"I don't want to go to Dallas. My doctor said, No flying!"

"You're kidding! Pregnant women fly all the time," he said continuing to type.

"Not so much ... in the last two months ..... the belly is so big ... it could explode!" using her hands to emphasize the explosion. "Pooowwww"

His eyes were as big as saucers, "No way! You have to stay here then!" He had finally heard something.

"I was joking, silly! But if I went into labor, I would be in a strange hospital ... I love my doctor and my hospital here!" she puckered her lips up as if pouting.

"You are in good shape and you walk every day and we... every night ... you are healthy enough. We can tie your legs together till we get back."

"Oh no! You did not say that?" Kyleigh was fuming.

"Okay, buddy! My legs are closed to you. You've made your bed now!" She returned with a pillow and sheets for him to sleep on the couch.

"I was making a joke, too! I meant if you close your legs real tight the baby will not fall out!" Guy was explaining.

She slammed the door and locked it to the bedroom. The dog was going wild.

She barked through the door, "You should have shut you mouth long ago and I am not talking about the dog."

He sat with the dog saying, "Mommy is real upset at daddy. I don't understand. It must be the hormone imbalance that I have heard sooooo much about. Geez!"

He went back to work and later, tried the door. It was locked.

"Honey, let me in … you know I can't sleep without! I need you! I love you!"

"Save it ... It won't work this time! You should have plead your case earlier. I'm in the bubble bath mood."

"Don't you dare. You might slip and fall, honey please! Let me in ..." he was trying to find the master key they had when they first moved in.

"If you are looking for that key, it is in my hand. Good night!"

"She meant it Velvet" He was walking to the couch that had a pull out bed. He could not open it. He tossed and turned at 4:30 AM, he was still awake. At 7:30 she emerged yawning, "What 'll it be?"

"Bacon and eggs," he said.

"What will the baby's name be?" she sighed.

"Madison Kyle Smith … I thought we agreed on that?"

"You never said we agreed." She was exhausted, she had been awake all night, too.

"That was the worst night. Tell me you will never lock me out again?" He was serious and down on his knees with his head on the child which on cue, kicked him.

"I never want to get that mad. You must listen to me. You want me to talk then you shut me out! I can't handle it!" She was crying and all night revenge tactics had back fired.

"I just don't know what came over me. I will call my doctor for an appointment," she said.

It had never occurred to him it maybe related to her trauma.

Hindsight was a teacher. She had been tied up by Jared Banks' goons.

He should have known better than saying we can "tie your legs together."

He was just not thinking as far as Kyleigh goes, it will never be a problem again. She will always have his undivided attention in the future.

He hugged her and said simply, "I'm sorry."

They went to her psychiatric appointment that afternoon. They had slept together for the first time without making love.

Doctor Washu confirmed, what he thought . The flashbacks came when he said tying her legs. Guy felt like he had been stabbed in the chest.

Her doctor asked, "How do you feel about it now?"

"I know he was ... but I was so angry. I could not control my anger," Kyleigh admitted.

"I want you to know it is a step in healing. It is okay to feel angry. It has to come out. Never keep it inside."

"Guy do you understand what she is saying?" the doctor asked.

"I know she was mad as hell and had never locked me out of our bedroom," Guy looked straight at the doctor.

"She was not angry at you, Mr Smith. She was angry at the past." He did not want to elaborate because he could see that Guy knew.

"Kyleigh, Guy has anger, too."

Kyleigh had never thought of that.

"His anger is not at you, Kyleigh. His flashback is about you being harmed. You both can come to couples therapy.

If you feel the need or to my office whichever you feel will benefit you the most. I look forward to working with you."

They shook hands with the doctor and left calmer than when they arrived. At least, had a clearer view.

"Whenever you need to talk in the future, I will stop what I am doing. I make this promise to you," Guy said.

Until now, he thought her reaction yesterday was the pregnancy hormones at work.

"I should leave you alone while you are working. I promise not to interrupt in the future," she said.

Their communication was back and they promised to talk about everything as they did before the kidnapping.

Kyleigh had not talked in detail about what had happened to her. He had told her once, he did not think he could handle it.

She knew it. She had it tucked away. So she scheduled another appointment.

"You're sure you do not want me to come with you?" he asked.

"I am. I am okay as long as I am told this is normal." She held his face and said, "You deserve a normal wife. Sometimes I just don't feel normal … yesterday was one of those days. I did not want you to see me … not normal! That is why I locked the door," she cried into his chest.

He was holding her so tight, he loosened so he would not hurt the baby … "You are my everything! This happened for a reason. I had my priorities mixed up. This has taught me you are at the top of all my lists. You talked and said things I needed to hear, and I found out that MY anger is normal too!"

Madeline, Jana and Bruce met with his lawyer, Adriana. She was a tall lanky brunette dressed in a dark gray business suit. She wore no makeup and there was no need. Her complexion was flawless. She walked into the courtroom, all eyes were upon her. When she spoke there was no doubt that her eloquent speaking voice was an asset to any case that she presented.

She was asking the court for a continuance in Bruce's case and it was granted. The opposing lawyer was approaching the bench and requesting denial. He was visible perturbed at the outcome.

Jana thanked Adriana as did Bruce. Now he was going to ask about Unitus. She said she was working on it and Trevor's warden friend, Bernie had him in solitary confinement. Until he or the feds could get him out, he was safe. Bruce's mind knowing that was relieved.

Adriana told Bruce she looked forward to meeting his friend, Unitus. There was a twinkle in her eyes.

Jana smiled. Her intuition was Miss Lawyer was not as cold as she appeared. She had just dropped her guard. Only another woman like Jana, could pick up on it.

Jana thought she must be captivated by Unitus's appearance in one of his body-building photos. Bruce had given her the photos so there would be no mistake, whom they were to transfer. Unitus was a friend and a valuable member of his operative group. He was oblivious to what Jana had discovered.

She was so glad she had her husband for six more months. She would fill him in when they returned to the ranch, on what she suspected.

She, herself was a natural born matchmaker. If this woman got her husband off she was going to pursue this further, but for now she was going to put that seed in Bruce's mind, too.

He said, "Leave it be, Jana. Unitus is too smart for Lady Long Legs."

So Bruce had already given her a code name. She giggled because her legs were short. The way her Bruce liked them. He had once said, "Jana your legs are forever for me to delight in." She blushed when thinking about her honeymoon and how every aspect of those days kept flooding her mind.

He was so special. Her husband and his family were so special to her. She smiled at Madeline. This lady had taken her as her daughter-in-law without reservations. She would be forever indebted to her.

Madeline and Trevor had even invited her family for Christmas, but hey could not leave their business in the most productive time of the year. They promised to come in the off-season. They walked to the white limo and drove to meet Trevor. He was at the office talking to the accountants about their liquid assets and the financial state of GM & GS OIL REFINERIES. He was so relieved to see those three people. He hugged all three. "I think we did make a wise choice in Adriana. Shows you should not judge a book by its cover. Would you' all let me buy you some lunch?"

Bruce called Guy when he got home. He and Kyleigh were relieved. He could hear Kyleigh jokingly saying, "You're going with me to the hospital, Jana! Bruce and Guy can come later."

That was true Bruce. He would be there. He was so emotional that he handed the phone to his mother. He walked to Jana and buried his head in her chest. They waved to Trevor and walked to their room. He had never let anyone, but Jana see him like this.

The thought of his grandchild, his grandson's birth was overwhelming. For him to be a part of this was a miracle, "I just need a minute and I will be okay."

"I know you will darling. It has been a big day for us." He kissed her and they just laid on the bed and rested.

Mind, Body, and Soul sometimes just need a rest!

Roscoe got a call from Guy about the news. He said, "Thank God!"

Guy said, "You know I have to go to Dallas. Can Kyleigh stay with you two? She said she can't fly and I have to go. Some things I cannot do on the computer. This is one of them. I hope this will be my last trip away from her."

Roscoe said, "Of course! Kyleigh is Beatrice's biggest fan. Those two in the same house will be a blessing. She is as big as a house and she lets me know how painful it is … Kyleigh will be a good sounding board for her. Just tell my sister-in-law to bring a large pair of earplugs!"

"Earplugs did you say earplugs?" Beatrice was standing over her husband and steam was coming out of her ears.

"Just a phrase, Sweetums! Got to go, Guy!" ... click.

"Kyleigh is going to stay with us while Guy flies to Dallas on the selling thing … selling of his company. Is that okay with you? I told him it would be okay," she was standing way too close to him.

"Perfect I will have someone to talk ... to because I will have my earplugs in … when a certain person comes home from work each day," pointing to him.

Roscoe was not laughing now, as he had with Guy.

Best to not say a word, Roscoe was saying to himself. The more I say the worse it will get … but then I do love make up sex! "HMMM what a dilemma!"

"What dilemma?" Beatrice said as she was walking away from him.

"Oh Hello Dolly!" Did I really say that out loud. The pregnancy must have affect my mental capacity to filter my inner thoughts and my outer thoughts.

Pregnancy brain that's what I am SUFFERING from!

"Geez! What a mess!" there I go again.

"What's a mess?" here she is again on top of me. Don't you dare say that out loud self.

"The yard, dear. I think I will go rake the yard. It's a mess!" Roscoe mumbled.

"It's the dead of winter. So don't try that one. Come to mama and tell me what is wrong?" holding her arms out.

"Now that is more like it!" Roscoe tried to get his arms around her, but was unsuccessful.

"You wanted two rambunctious boys and you got them ... so deal with it big guy!"

She was grinning and batting those pale green eyelashes at him, "I need a good back rub Roscoe, darling … Please don't stop! Don't Stop!" She was teasing him unmercifully.

Those were the pre- pregnancy word he would tell her.

"Honey after the boys are born we will have much much make up sex," she said.

Now his eyes were sparkling she had hit the nail on the head. WOW! Was she a mind reader or what?

Kyleigh and Beatrice had been on the phone all afternoon and what they would do when Guy was gone to Dallas.

"Another thing ... I was told to bring earplugs. What do you need earplugs for?" Kyleigh asked.

"To put in my ears when Roscoe is pleading for me to have sex. What else could I use them for ... hmm let me think. I could tying them around his d--- and he could swing a pregnant woman around the house. Then I could have the room vacuumed in no time flat. What do you think my dear friend?" Beatrice concluded.

Roscoe was making a sandwich and he dare not look at his wife, "I'm off to work. See you when I get home," running to the Silverado.

"Boy I thought the first three months was the worst of it. No one told me about the last three months. Wonder why? Guess it is best that I don't impart this wisdom to any younger guys. Yep! Something I am gonna keep to myself."

He was still talking to himself when he pulled up in the driveway at work. Inscoe said, "Who are you talking to?"

"I was on my blue-tooth, Smarty!" and he got out of the truck to square off with Inscoe.

He was not intimidated, "You don't have one, Roscoe! How is it in paradise?" his friend was making a point and standing way too close.

He could easily knock his block off. Hey wait a minute self. Are you crazy? He is your friend.

"I think I have pregnancy brain, Inscoe," shaking his head up and down.

Adding by stretching his neck and swallowing hard, "Yes, you warned me … I guess … it is just something you have to learn for yourself ...Pregnant ...Women can change overnight! What am I saying?" they were walking to the building.

Turning to Inscoe, "Every hour … every hour. Did I say every second?" They both laughed and went inside.

The day got better … Inscoe told him he had something to tell him at the end of the day.

"You are not quitting are you?" Roscoe queried.

"NO. Something worse! Dang! I might as well tell you... Cindy is pregnant!"

His wife is pregnant. They walked to Roscoe's office and closed the door. He hugged his friend and patted him on the back. "Congrats! How old is your youngest? Twenty two ...WOW... I didn't realize this could go on forever."

"I should have got them snipped, but she kept saying I just want one more. That was ten years ago," Inscoe smiled.

"I am happy for you Roscoe and I make fun … but it is the best experience you will ever have Roscoe ... when you see your babies for the first time. You will forget about today. Trust me!" Inscoe was imparting his wisdom to Roscoe. He really needed to hear that today.

"MEN do chatter like WOMEN!" Frida was telling the other ladies in the building."Yes I heard it on the intercom … it was not like I was snooping or anything. He left it on … what was I suppose to do ... Not listen?" they laughed.

Roscoe spoke to Frida's intercom, "You need to buy a set of EARPLUGS … Take it out of petty cash!"

CHAPTER THREE

It was the middle of February and the lawyers had finally sealed a deal. Trevor and Madeline told Guy on the phone it was a fair deal and they had held out to see if the billionaire would pay more. It was the max and would pay no higher and they would keep their stocks in the company at 40 % that was agreeable, and he was to fly out tomorrow. The 60 % would make the company a killing.

Madeline had negotiated as her husband Sam had taught her. Trevor let her do the wheeling and dealing because it gave him great pleasure to watch her.

He knew the billionaire personally from his childhood and a simple handshake would have been sufficient.

Guy had taken Kyleigh and her dog to Beatrice's and Roscoe had drove him in the Silverado to the airport. The mountains had snow on them, but the Charlotte Airport was clear.

The small company airplane had no problem getting airborne and Guy was going to miss the luxury of the GM & GS Oil Refineries airplane. He would get another.

No worries. The only worry was Kyleigh. He prayed she

did not have their son while he was gone. He did not want to miss a minute of their happiness.

Madeline and Trevor met him at the airport. It was clear and sunny skies in Dallas. The limo drove them to the ranch and they grilled a steak and ate a leisurely supper. They spent the evening talking about the impending sell.

They would go in the morning, and it would be a done deal.

GS read all the papers, and agreed it was a fair deal.

Madeline ask him, if he wanted to change anything and he said, "It is perfect GM" she kissed him on the back of his neck when she passed his chair.

"I am going to check on dessert," she said walking from the outdoor kitchen into the house.

Bruce and Jana had eaten with them, and Jana had followed her into the kitchen. Jana had saw that Madeline had paled.

"Are you okay?" Madeline was holding firmly to the counter top.

"I am afraid my cancer had come back. I dare not tell Trevor or Guy and please don't tell Bruce. I will make an appointment as soon as this is over. Soon as the babies come!" She took some tablets from her purse.

"Are you sure it is wise to wait?"

"I have my priorities set. I will be fine. Thanks you, Hon for listening." Jana ordered her to sit and watch while she prepared the strawberry shortcake which was the men's favorite dessert.

She asked the MEN to bring it out. Madeline had gone to the bathroom. Madeline had entrusted her with this secret. She had always been able to keep a secret. She was not sure if she could keep this one.

They sat eating and talking. She smiled at Madeline who said it was delicious. "Jana fixed it!" I am teaching her the Western desserts you MEN like."

Bruce thought Jana is too quiet and that is not a good sign.

She had been too cheerful until tonight. What was wrong? It had something to do with either Guy or Madeline.

Guy went to his old room and called Kyleigh. She and Beatrice were having a blast. He could see it on his phone. He could tell by the merriment in his wife's voice.

"You should have seen us trying to get up the staircase. We finally gave up. Me and Beatrice will have to make a tepee out back, and sleep on the ground. We are so uncomfortable and so big, we waddle. It won't make any difference as long as we don't have to climb stairs."

Kyleigh took a breath and asked, "How was your day my husband?" smiling into the phone.

He kissed the phone and Beatrice said, "You two stop that! Roscoe is not home yet! I can't handle X-rated movies unless he is home," they all laughed. Beatrice was a character. She always made you laugh.

Roscoe was home now and he sure was glad to hear the laughter. The two dogs met him at the door. Kyleigh was kissing her phone as Beatrice came to meet him.

"They are playing kissy face. Want some?" BeBe asked.

Roscoe's brows were going up and down, "Have I ever refused?" They kissed in the hallway and it was great. "Can Kyleigh live here? I loved the way you just welcomed me home."

Arms around his neck, "We will have to ask Guy when he comes home. I have always liked kissy-face!" kissing him again.

Kyleigh came around the corner, "If I can't ... you can't!"

"Sorry ... How is the Bro?" Roscoe asked keeping Beatrice figure between him and Kyleigh.

Beatrice put one hand behind her while she was talking to Kyleigh, and Roscoe was making all sorts of faces.

Kyleigh asked,"Did I miss something? Are you okay Roscoe?" He straightened and took both of Beatrice's hands and folded them in front of her."I'm fine." Beatrice knew he was not OK.

She could feel the problem in the middle of her back, "Oh my Lord, Roscoe can you help me fold some clothes?" She would have to walk him to the laundry room.

Kyleigh said, "You two stop! I am on to you. Guy would love to have a foursome, but no you two wait till he is thousands miles away to fold your clothes!"

"I will find my phone and take a picture of you two folding clothes, then he will wish he had stayed at home."

They were all laughing and the dogs barking. They were all having fun .... until Kyleigh's water broke.

Swoosh and it went everywhere! The floor was wet and slippery. "Don't anyone of you fall! You women sit!"

"OH HELLO DOLLY!" Is all Roscoe could say!

He went to steady her. "You are okay? Now just lay down on the couch ... while I call the doctor" ... He can meet us at the hospital in fifteen minutes, the doctor said.

"Don't call Guy! He has that meeting tomorrow. After the meeting you can tell him anything. This may take a long time.

The doctor said it usual took a long time for the first one. I'm fine! She laid down and a contraction hit her. She was squealing.

"Get your watch Beatrice ... and write down this time and how long it last!" He had the doctor on the phone and the dogs were whining.

"Hold on Doc! Beatrice put the dogs in the crates! Hello Dr Bass ... I am trying to not get eaten alive . . . Oh yes! I have the right number. I am calling for Kyleigh Smith . . . Her water broke at my house. Her husband is out of town and she is staying with me ..... and my wife." He was rambling, but doing the best he could.

When this happened in the past as a police officer, he was calm, cool, and collected, but he DIDN'T know the people! It does make a difference. This was his sister-in-law.

"OH MY LORD! Doc, she is screaming again. They are twenty-five minutes apart. We will be there in a few!" Dr Bass said he would meet them at the hospital.

Beatrice was wiping sweat from Kyleigh's brow.

"James bring the limo. Kyleigh is having the baby! I can't get her in the truck without hurting her. Drive safely!" There was still snow on the mountain. He would call ahead and make sure the snowplow was in the area.

"Inscoe get the highway patrol and a snowplow to my house NOW!" Roscoe's thoughts were... "If anything happens to Kyleigh . . . Guy will kill me."

Kyleigh said not to call him, "What should I do Lord?"

He told Beatrice, "When we get to the hospital, and the doctor tells me when the baby will arrive, I will call grandma and she can be my buffer!"

Beatrice said, "Let your conscience be your guide. If I was delivering, would he call you? Damn, straight! But you do what you think is best!"

He put a call in and Kyleigh was wailing in agony. Beatrice

told him to go outside and talk. The patrol was here, and the snowplow he could see in the distance. It was going to be a long night. It was late, midnight here so it was 8:00PM there.

Trevor answered, "Kyleigh's water broke and I am in the process of getting her to the hospital. Snow is on the ground ans the snowplow has just arrived. You all do what you have to but I had to call. Tell Guy! I got to go!"

Every twenty minutes Kyleigh let out a blood-curdling scream. The dogs were going crazy, they may hurt themselves. He went and talked baby talk to them, and gave them some steak and they were happy til she screamed again!

The limo was here and they wrapped Kyleigh in a blanket, and Roscoe toted her to the car. "She is light as a feather," looking at Beatrice.

It took FOREVER to get to the hospital.

"Beatrice are you okay?" Roscoe asked and she nodded.

"Honey please don't you both go into labor at the same time. My heart can't take the stress," Roscoe saw the look on her face … "I'm kidding. Are you hurting?"

"I'm fine," Beatrice reassured him.

Kyleigh was now screaming every fifteen minutes.

Beatrice was holding her hands, and rubbing them and having her pant like a puppy.

"LaMaze instructor where are you?" BeBe asked.

""Not in here!" James said. "We are almost there."

She was so pale, the pain had drained her. It was freezing outside and she was sweating profusely.

Roscoe asked, "Why is she so sweating so much?"

Beatrice looked at him in her own special way, "If you were squeezing a watermelon through your peter, MY darling! You would be sweating, too!" She didn't say dummy! He nodded.

The Dallas Fort Worth Airport was now snowed in and no flight could go out or come in until further notice.

Trevor had called ahead before Madeline called Guy. The way it was snowing he had a feeling. It would probably be clear by morning and he would tell Guy that. He doubted Guy would hear him.

Bruce was told first. "You may have to sit on him." Trevor and Bruce nodded. Guy walked in the room of all solemn faces and Jana was cowering in the corner. He knew it was something happening and he was going to find out what.

"It's Kyleigh, isn't it?" GM turned her head and looked out the window.

He was beginning to tremble uncontrollably, "Tell me and tell me now!"

Bruce said, "She is fine. She has gone into labor. Roscoe and Beatrice have got her to the hospital, son."

Guy screamed that was so visceral that no one in the room could comfort him."I knew it! I was so busy making this deal, I didn't put her first again," pacing like a caged animal.

"She needs me! Call the lawyer. I will give him my verbal power of attorney for you to sign, GM," he paced.

"Get me a plane! I am gone!"

He went to leave the room and Trevor said, "Now son, I have called for you ... but they are letting no planes in or out in this storm. The pilot said as soon as he got clearance, he would call me, and you will be on your way!"

He hit the door so hard it splintered it. He walked out in the snow ... he felt as helpless as he had when Jared Banks had his wife. There was nothing he could do then and nothing he could do now.

Trevor followed him outside and took him a coat. "You have to take care of yourself .... If you get a cold, they will not let you into the nursery."

"You are right ... I am not thinking clearly." He put it on and a hat, and walked around in circles, beating himself up. Trevor let him walk awhile and then he asked, "Would you like to go in my office and Skype Kyleigh?" he said nothing.

"You can be with her ... like the guys are overseas ... they are in the delivery rooms with their wives," he still hadn't said anything ... just walked to the house.

So he had at least heard what Trevor had said, then he answered him.

"Trevor I just don't know. If I can handle her hurting, and I cannot be there to comfort her."

"Guy she will be comforted ... if she can see your face."

"We are behind you whatever you decide," Trevor hugged him and he hugged Trevor.

He called Roscoe, and Beatrice answered. She is still in the labor room. The doctor sent me out and Roscoe has gone to get some coffee.

"I want to talk to her … I want to see her … the airport is shut down. I have to tell her I will be there as soon as I can... he started sobbing.

Beatrice said, "I will ask the doctor now. Here comes Roscoe," she flung the phone at him forgetting Guy could see.

"Sorry hon, I dropped the phone."

She went into the labor room, "Tell Guy I will ask the doctor, if he can Skype her, Okay?"

Roscoe told Guy, "It just happened so fast. Her water broke and we got the patrol and snowplow and got her here!"

"Thank you! I owe you one ...two, I can't count now! This is killing me!"

"I know Bro … I know! If it was me, you'd do the same! She's in good hands! Beatrice will be back in just a minute … If anyone crosses her … she is big enough to bulldoze them!"

Guy was killing himself laughing … and Beatrice was not amused … "I heard that you guys!" glaring at Roscoe.

"Yes! I bulldozed the entire labor room," and she blew on her knuckles and rubbed them on her breasts.

She grabbed the phone, "I will take you to see our girl … reminder she is hurting every five to ten minutes. This is normal! She is having contractions. So talk fast and don't hang up! You may see your son soon ... Love you! .... Got to waddle," holding the phone up high so he could see her exaggerated waddle.

"Waddle waddle waddle ... Here you go Kyleigh! It's your husband, honey!"

She was crying and sweating and begging... "Please give me something for pain … Guy tell them to give me something PLEASE," she was screaming and he was clenching his fists.

"Honey I love you … do that panting thing ....

She said, "You you do it with me," and they did. "HEE HEE blow! HEE HEE blow!" as they are doing this …

The doctor said, "I can't give her anymore of the pain med. It could stop the birth and too much may hurt the baby..."

Kyleigh looked at the doctor and said, "You didn't tell me that! I don't want anything then! Watch out Guy I am going to explode." She started pushing and pushing...

The doctor got under her and the baby was out! He held the baby up and suctioned him and Guy heard the baby cry!

They weighed him, foot printed him, and swaddled him. Then they gave him back to Kyleigh for her to show him ...

"AWWWWW!"

"Everyone come here and meet Madison Kyle Smith!"

"He is sooo beautiful like you are … my darling! As soon as this airport is clear. I will be on my way home. I will NEVER leave you again!"

"Take your time honey ... I got a feeling I am going to sleep for a week!"

"That's okay! I'll kiss you awake! Till then use your phone!"

Beatrice said, "Roscoe call my doctor!" they had just got on the elevator.

"You are kidding, right?"

She shook her head... "No, I have been in pain all day! I can't wait much longer!"

He picked her up and went back to the delivery room …

"HEEELLLLPPPPPP!"

Thirty minutes later … One boy arrived … three minutes later another boy arrived and two minutes later. They were picking Roscoe up off the floor.

By then Beatrice had one baby boy under each arm, "Ammonia does the body good! Right Roscoe? You are my hero!"

"Nah ... you are my hero! You can bulldoze over me anytime!"

"Whoa! Kiss me lightly or I may pop another one out!"

His eyes were big as saucers, "For Real?"

Tate had got a job shoveling snow from the front of houses. He made enough money to buy some new clothes for school.

The girls at school were circling, but Debbie stood out in his mind.

She had told him that he would remember her and he sure had. There she was in front of his locker.

He asked, "Are you still mad?"

She said, "Don't flatter yourself." She had stretch jeans on that hugged her figure in all the right places. He was kicking himself for not tasting the goods, but he was not going backwards anymore.

She was giggling with a bunch of girls. He was getting his books out and he felt they were laughing at him. He took his math book out and a naked picture of her fell out of his book. His mouth flew open.

He walked over to her and said, "Nice try!"

He was doing too good in school to get kicked out.

He had read her right the first go round. Every bone in his body was aching for her and the pathetic thing was she knew it. Those eyes were staring at him and she was rubbing her hands up and down her legs as she sat at the table.

Run... dummy... run. He asked the teacher if he could be excused that he had a bad headache and needed to go home.

She gave him a pass and he went by the office and left the building. When he got home, there she was sitting on his bed.

She said, "What took you so long?"

"Are you for real? My aunt will be here any minute!"

"And you will be in a heap of trouble bringing me home to have your way with … she won't like that!"

"You are one evil b---!" he mumbled the words.

She came closer, "Why don't you give me what I want and then I'll go!"

"And what do you want?" he wanted to be very clear about what she was asking.

"I want you to be my man in school and out of school and I will treat you like a king … nothing more... nothing less. Do you think you can handle me? Or not?"

"You want protection from a dude right?" "You want to see my ass get beat and that is the bottom line."

She had tears in her eyes, "Yes he won't leave me alone and he tells me horrible things he is going to do to me. I am terrified!"

"Why not go to the police?" he suggested.

"I can't my father would kill me! He'd say it was all my fault. He is always harping on me about the way I dress. I dress this way to irritate him ... It is the only time he talks to me … to criticize me!"

"Who is the dude you are frightened of?"

"Lester on the football team. He swore he will rape me the first chance he gets. He and the team have gang raped two girls I know, and the school will not do anything, and the police don't believe them."

"OK I will help you, but you got to get some clothes to cover up. What is with the photo in my book?"

"I wanted you to see what you are getting into. Coraine is one of the girls the team raped. That is why she is so screwed up. I have listened to her and I do not judge her."

"What is your last name Debbie?"

"Fletcher," she said.

"Can you kiss me like you mean it? So when we are in public I won't go to pieces?" she licked her lips.

"If you play me I will do more than rape you. I will whip your ass. Understand?"

"Understood!" He grabbed her by the neck and put his tongue half way down her throat. She just stood very still. He pulled her to him and cupped both buttocks and drew her to him entirely. She did not flinch. He thought I must be doing something wrong. This girl is made of STONE.

"I was the other girl that they gang raped. I have no feelings left. I just don't want to die."

Then he held her close without fondling. She was fragile or she was a good liar. He knew how it was to be afraid and beaten to a pulp. He would protect her as best as he could, but the football team would be after him. If they wanted to abuse her again, he knew it was going to mean trouble. Trouble was all he had known all his life.

He had met a friend at the library. His name was Roscoe. He may just ask him for some help with this situation.

He took her by the hand and walked her to the library.

Roscoe was not there. He asked what Roscoe's last name was. They told him Smith. He owns the Smith Security. You know the tall building a couple of blocks from here.

"OK Thanks!"

"Do you want to walk with me there or do you want me to walk you home?"

"Walk me home, please!" she started crying uncontrollably. He got her a paper towel and gave it to her.

"I have no clue why I am crying. It just happens sometimes. You are being too nice. I am sorry, if I embarrassed you. The picture is one they took of me, and passed it around the whole school so no one would talk to me, but Coraine."

"It's true. I didn't understand my cousin until now. I do a little better. I … too, was judging her."

They walked to her house a small one like Aunt Eunice's. She waved and went inside.

He did have a headache and no homework done. He could still feel her against him. It was the first girl he had had in his arms, and he had not laid.

The papers were signed and Guy was on the runway waiting for takeoff, now that the runway was clear. Bruce and Jana were with him. They were going to stay at Trevor's Southfork in Hendersonville. Hoping to see the new grandson.

Jana told him that she would be able to help Kyleigh and Beatrice when they got home from the hospital. He was so thankful.

"You know I have no idea what to do with a new baby. We were going to classes, but that is not like the real thing. Dad did you know how to change a diaper?"

"No your mother and grandmother did all that, but if Jana teaches me. No problem!" Bruce said.

"You guys had better be prepared for the crying. That's what I am told. I have never been a mother, but I will learn as we go, too." Looking into Bruce's eyes, "I love you two very much."

Kyleigh was asleep when they got there. The nurse said she had had a rough night and had just gone to sleep. So they walked to the nursery. There was the little prince. Madison Kyle Smith was asleep, too! They just oohed and aahed at the nursery window.

Then they saw Roscoe come around the corner. He was on the way to the nursery to see his boys.

Guy hugged him and thanked him, "Thank God she was at your house. I can't imagine her being alone and this happening."

"It was touch and go with the roads. A real nightmare, but we made it. The highway patrol we must thank and that snowplow guy. I'd like to do something nice for both of them!"

"You say what and I will have it delivered this morning. Let's see your boys. I just saw mine.

Roscoe hugged Bruce and Jana. They looked in on Cain and Caleb. They were dressed in blue and in a double crib. "There's my boys asleep as is Beatrice. What do you think about getting some of the wonderful cafeteria breakfast?"

They all laughed and got on the elevator and went down to eat and get some hot steaming coffee. "Remind me to take Kyleigh some. She has missed her coffee something awful!" Guy laughed.

Bruce was beaming at Guy. "You did good son. He is

a beautiful baby and Roscoe's twins will be their cousin's security team. These three boys will rule the world. That I foresee."

Guy and Roscoe in unison, "Here!Here!" cheer. The whole cafeteria was looking at them as if they had loss their minds.

Guy had brought a box of cigars in . The "No Tobacco" sign was up meant nothing to him. He asked Roscoe, "As long as we don't light up. Right?" "You have to ask the nurse. I have no jurisdiction here!" Roscoe said.

"Nurses rule here!" Roscoe grinned.

Madeline and Trevor met with Marcus Buchanan after Guy left. They decided to have dinner together at Abacus-Dallas around 6:00 PM.

The billionaire insisted on footing the bill and wanted to catch up on Trevor's life.

"Trevor I have missed you, my friend. Your wife looks ravishing tonight!"

Madeline smiled and Trevor said, "OK Marc put those eyes back in your head! She is mine and don't you forget it!" They all laughed.

She had on an Oscar de la Renta creation of sapphire that slit up the back. The lines were straight across the shoulders and had an empire waistline. On her six foot frame, it dazzled the eye. The three-inch Louis Vuitton silver anklet strapped heels made he tower over the short man, Buchanan. She was Trevor's equal in every way and he knew it. Buchanan just had to test the water. He never met a woman he could not buy till now.

Her hair and makeup was done to perfection by her friend that came to the house. Trevor had not seen her in this light for a while and he knew she had gone the extra mile to make him proud.

He was beaming and whispered in her ear, "I love you in cowboy boots and jeans the best." That melted her heart."You love me is all that matters. This fancy stuff is not for me, but I know you think a lot of Marcus and it was a profitable day."

He pulled the chair out for her to sit and Marcus ordered the nine course tasting for all. "This is why I come here. The food is fabulous."

They chatted and talked about the grand babies. "Yep! I'm a great grandpa. You have any grandchildren?" Trevor asked. Marcus reviewed the list of six wives, three children, five grandchildren and two greats. "But sad to say I am without a spouse at the moment. Haven't found the right woman to tame my pocketbook … yet?"

They laughed but Madeline thought it sad. She was looking into Trevor's eyes and he could see she was a happy woman. He felt blessed.

They left around ten and said their goodbyes knowing this was not their circle of fun, and knew their paths would probably not meet again. It was the end of GM & GS Oil Refineries and the beginning of their life back in Hendersonville. She looked at Trevor and said, "We can now go home where our heart is. Tomorrow I will begin packing."

He said, "You will not my love." She did a double take in the limo. "Whatever do you mean?"

"We are sleeping late tomorrow," looking deep into her eyes. "I will hire someone to come in and pack everything. They will deliver and set it up in three day and my wife will not be tired. You have been looking very tired lately."

She said to herself she would make an appointment at Duke as soon as they got back to Hendersonville. Her husband was too observant. She must and when settled, would talk to him about what she suspected.

"It's been a long day, Trev I'm fine."

"Are you just sad about the business?"

"I am actually relieved that it is over and done. One less thing to worry about. Now I can focus on you," and she smiled that smile that he loved.

"Now that is what I like to hear!" He placed her hand in his. They sat looking out the skylight roof and relaxing.

As the starlight were twinkling, and the bright city lights were fading in the distance.

PART EIGHT

CHAPTER ONE

Unitus had been set free and he called his friend Bruce, "Thanks, buddy! I know you got me out. So where are you?"

"I'm in Hendersonville, a little town in North Carolina. You have never heard of it, but don't bring your sorry ass down here. I got my Jana and my grandson was just born."

"You a grandpa … Congrats! So glad for you."

Jana said, "Tell him," poking Bruce in his ribs.

"MY wife is playing matchmaker. She wants me to tell you that my lawyer in Dallas has the HOTS for you. Now I have said it, she will leave me alone."

"She is poking me again. Her name is Adriana Buchanan and believe me ... she is hot. Ouch! Jana just took the side of my head off so she still loves me!" laughing into the phone and kissing his wife.

"The only thing that worries me this woman is not a bimbo. She is so smart she may break your heart, my friend! Let me know if you test the waters, and if you do hook up, I will see you at the courthouse in about six months. It is time you settled down, Unitus. It is nothing like it, not …. anything!" Jana was poking him again.

Beatrice had walked to Kyleigh's hospital room and sat down.

"I have a very important question to ask you," Kyleigh said with a puzzled look on her face. "How did you have two babies in thirty minutes and it took me all day to have one!"

Beatrice reared back in the recliner and said nonchalantly, "Well let me see ... you didn't have three months puking as I did ... so I guess it was in the stars that something equaled it out!"

Kyleigh screwed her mouth up like Elvis and said, "Hmm three months versus one day that seems about fair!" and they were both laughing when the husbands came in the room with much needed coffee.

Guy was kissing Kyleigh, Roscoe was kissing Beatrice, and Bruce was kissing Jana when the nurse walked in, and the nurse walked out. She said to the other nurses, "There's a real orgy going on in there." They all ran to see the couples making out.

"Oh my goodness ...This family is going to visit us quite often!" one nurse said.

"Yep looks like to me ... they don't know what is going to happen when they get home with these crying babies. Let them have their fun here!" said the older nurse pointing to this hospital room.

Soon the room was filled with babies and their moms nursing them. The nurses were instructing them about nipple care and the men sauntered on out the door.

No construction had been done on the boathouse and dock due to the recent snowfall. The stables however, had been completed. The heating and air- conditioning for the horses and precious dogs were being installed tomorrow.

Trevor had been on the phone all morning to make sure it was completed before they transported the dogs on the plane.

He had rented furniture in the Hendersonville Southfork and wanted to get the movers underway by the end of the week. He wanted his own furniture.

He missed his desk and all his secret communication devices were going to have to be installed exactly like his Dallas home. That major detail he had taken care of at both residences.

He spoke to Bruce and informed him of the projects so he could oversee them until they returned.

Madeline was still curled up in bed. Enjoying not having to be in the office early. She had packed her few possessions at GM & GS Oil Refineries. They had been delivered this morning, that way the moving company could ship them with the furniture.

"All systems are running smoothly darling." He laid beside her and asked, "Are you feeling okay?"

"I'm just resting up for those three great grand kids. If we fly back by the end of the week, there will be no rest for the weary!"

"But they have parents, and Bruce and Jana will help them, all while you and I stay in the background with Blackie & Black Magic, they are our babies."

"You are right we are over-the-hill and through the woods. We are so close, if they need us they will call. I have to learn how to let go. You are teaching me. I am just a slow learner."

"You are not slow about anything," Trevor was definitely enjoying her being home all day.

Madeline looked into his eyes and said, "It is a good thing I cannot have any more children or we would probably have triplets by now," wrapping a long leg across him and he growled.

Bruce and Jana were taking care of the boys two dogs, Dynamite & Black Velvet. They had been warned about holding and screaming. Bruce told Jana not to make him scream tonight and she swatted him with her snow gloves.

They were driving on back to the ranch, when a black bear crossed the road in front of them. Bruce swerved and missed him. The mountains were full of wildlife, but that animal was something that would make Jana scream. She did and shivered, Bruce folded her under his arm and said, "Nothing is going to hurt you my baby! Relax and talk to me about that beautiful grandson we have. If I was not married to a stubborn woman, I would not have seen him. I love your stubbornness. You never give up that is why we match so well. I never give up either. Are you asleep?"

She was sound asleep. He carried her to their bedroom undressed her and pulled the covers up. By the time he had showered, she was awake and stretching like a tigress. Those dark brown slanted eyes with gold specks were intensely focused on him. She crawled on all four to the edge of the bed where he stood.

She pulled at the robe's belt until she had it open and fell to the floor. He had not moved.

She licked his thighs. He closed his eyes and grabbed her hair, but just to massage her scalp. She licked his navel and up to his nipples and tasted gently and up to his neck until she was standing, and could enter his left ear with her tongue and whispered, "Did you leave me naked for a reason?"

She had her nipples rubbing against his chest, he did not respond. He began massaging her buttocks and pulling her onto him. She was losing her breath so she breathed more deeply. She fondled him, and he moaned.

"You make me so happy I don't want to waste a minute. You don't have to wear clothes here EVER in our room. You can lick, taste and tease all you want. Climb me I am ready! For anything you want me to do," and she did.

The heat and air-conditioning was installed the next morning and Bruce called Trevor to let him know.

"Thank you for taking care of that for me! We will be coming in about 4:00PM on Friday. That way the dogs are settled before dark. "When are the babies coming home? Wednesday that will be good. We won't have to sit at the hospital and have to wait to see them amongst the crowd at the nursery window. Kiss Jana for us and we will see you Friday!" Trevor was glad they were there to watch the place for them.

The security guards were watching all the houses while the families were at the hospital all day. Roscoe and Guy were riding in together and two days their brotherly parties at night would be over.

Roscoe heard one of the teenagers at the library and had been to the office wanting to talk to him. He left his name Tate and phone number. This was a good time to touch base with him. He liked the kid.

"Hi Roscoe! Thank you for calling. I can't talk in front of the family. This is a personal matter about, "cupping the phone and whispering,"A GIRL", Tate said.

Roscoe was respectful, "I understand. WE have just had twin boys. They will be coming home Wednesday and crying so why don't you come by the hospital anytime tomorrow. We can go in a quiet room here and talk. Unless you need to talk now?"

"No, tomorrow will be fine. See you when I get out of school. The person with me may need to talk to you anyways. Thanks so much. Just didn't know which way to turn," click.

"Poor kid. His brother was raising him is now in jail and pawned him off on his aunt who already has four children of her own," Roscoe said.

"Where'd you meet him Bro?" Guy was putting ice on his head where he bumped it on Kyleigh's bed.

"Where did you get that goose egg?"

Guy frowned and said,"Don't ask!"

"I met him at the library. He is working hard to keep up his grades so he can go to college. Now it seems he has girl trouble and who'd he want to call? Yea, Ghostbuster me!" Roscoe was grinning.

"He thinks I have all the answers because I once was a police officer. He is so wrong. I just know if Beatrice had not come to that wedding and swept me off my flat feet, I would be calling a Ghostbuster named GUY!

They were laughing and yawning.

"I think I will call it a day. We have only one more day of freedom Bro!" Guy was headed for bed and so was Roscoe.

"Night Ghostbuster!" said Guy.

"Nite Ghostbuster!" said Roscoe.

CHAPTER TWO

Roscoe took Beatrice some sunflowers and Guy took Kyleigh some lavender flowers. The girls were once again giggling. That meant, they were getting better.

They had nursed the babies and Roscoe said while they were alone, "I have to admit this to you, honey!"

"You have had an affair," she teased.

"NO, not that! ....That I am jealous!" he lowered his eyes.

"Jealous?" frowning she said.

"Of my boys," still looking down at his chest.

"What do you mean?" she asked puzzled.

"I want to suck them. Yum Yum Yum."

She threw her pillow at him, "Glutton!"

"Okay come to mama and suckle away but the boys will starve, and they will have you up for child abuse. "I'll take my chances," and kissed everything, but her nipples. "OH Roscoe you know what we missed out on?" She was writhing as if in pain from sexual starvation.

"What, Hon?"

"We were going to have sex all the way to the delivery room!" "If you keep doing that you may be pregnant before we leave here. So STOP, woman! I will promise next time we will do what you just said!" he had crossed his legs and was squeezing them together.

She stopped, and sat up and said, "Okay!" need was gone.

Bruce and Jana walked in with Guy. Jana said. "We will wait out in the waiting room while you and Kyleigh have some time together. Just holler when you want a visit. They wanted to sneak to the nursery.

Kyleigh was smiling and had her arms out, "I am ready for my big fat juicy kiss for breakfast,"

"OH MY LORD ... you are horny!"

"No, I just miss you and the other thing, it maybe awhile. I have 42 stitches and it maybe awhile, but I heal real fast. I know how to please my man, in other ways," batting her eye- lashes.

"You sure do, darling! Let's change the subject for now." He was breathing real fast and she was pulling him down to kiss her. She began sucking on his tongue.

"You do that again and I might burst your stitches and they'll have to operate on me and you both who would take care of Madison?"

"Jana," she said.

"I know she would, my darling," Guy licked his lips.

"No, Guy. She is behind you!" There Bruce and Jana stood.

"Like father like son!" Jana said. "Pay no attention to these two. How are you feeling, my dear?"

For a five foot woman, she had an presence of authority, and the two men took a seat.

Kyleigh said, "I feel like a semi truck ran over me, but when I am better you must teach me that maneuver."

Tate phoned Roscoe he was on the maternity floor. He came around the corner and shook his hand and shook Debbie's hand.

He asked the nurse if there was a place where they could talk privately.

"Sure," and lead them to a vacant consultation room.

Tate and Debbie sat very close. Roscoe noticed she was squeezing Tate's hand and appeared to be frightened. Of what? He hoped to find out soon.

"Thank you man, I just don't know how to handle this situation. WE need some advice. Debbie will tell you what happened to her, and then I will tell you what I have agreed to do for her."

Roscoe wanted to ask if she was pregnant, but he didn't.

He just sat and listened, nodding and frowning as they told their stories.

He gritted his teeth when she got to the gang-rape, and the football team and the school's omission of reporting and convicting the punks. Tate was an unusually sensitive kid.

Since Roscoe himself was adopted, thanks heavens he had found a real family to love him.

Tate said he had found a real family at his aunt's house. He wanted to help the kid and the girl has no one. Her father doesn't believe her and she has been through too much and survived.

"This has got to be reported to the authorities," he said. She laughed, "I did but they didn't believe me."

She began to cry BIG crocodile tears. "She cries a lot with no warning," he said as she was blowing her nose and Tate had his arm around her.

"How can I help her, Roscoe? Knowing these goons will

break my face and have me expelled from school. I will lose my scholarship. Make no mistake I will fight them, if they try to hurt her. You see why I need your advice."

"I am glad you came to me. We will get you some help Debbie. You need to be in a battered SHELTER for the time being. First is to keep you safe. Did you have any witnesses?"

"Tate's cousin Coraine. They raped her, too. She has not told her mother. She is using drugs to deal with it! I just can't because my mother died from a drug overdose, and that is why my dad hates me. He thinks I am just like her," she said.

"I was at her house when I met Tate and asked him to help me," she added. "He doesn't need to get hurt on my account," She was crying again. Tate was hugging her.

Roscoe said, "I have a security service and I will provide protection for both of you. Will you go into a shelter? Your choice."

"Can Tate visit me?" she begged.

"I can arrange a visit after we get the goons into custody. Till then he needs to stay away from you. The team may not just beat him up. They may kill him. Will you testify and put them away so they cannot hurt another young girl or young boy?"

"Yes," Debbie said.

Then you have to go tonight. You can tell no one not even your father. The shelter will furnish or my wife will get you some clothes. MY sister-in-law was brutalized, you may have read it in the papers, but she got help and you may need therapy as she did. She is now married and has just had a baby. So there can be a happy ending."

"Give me a few minutes and I will get this ball a rolling." They sat there holding each other. Not talking. He talked to the nurse and told her these kids need to stay in that room that he would be back to get them.

He had his team on the job and he talked to one of his old police officers. A genuine good guy that would help with the paperwork and the procedures to follow.

He went to Beatrice and told her what was happening.

She said, "Go and do what you got do, Big Guy!" she kissed him and he was gone.

Tate and Debbie walked with him to the security car and they got in. It was going to be a long night. They dropped Tate off so he would not know where they were going. He just knew Roscoe was going to keep her safe. He kissed her on her cheek and said, "You hang in there. Talk to you soon."

He went into the house and started studying. The only way to keep his mind off of her and keep anyone in the house from asking questions.

"Leave me alone. I am studying!"

Janie Andrews, Social Worker drove them to the shelter and she assured Roscoe, she would be safe. He gave Debbie his phone number encase she needed anything. He gave her a prepaid phone. She did not have a phone like most teenagers. He told her to keep it locked up when showering and in her bra doing the day. Janie talked to her at length about her rape, etc.

Roscoe was on his way back to the hospital to see his family.

He had to talk to Guy and Bruce. He may need the family to help with this one. He knew when Trevor and grandma got back, GM would sink her teeth into this one.

Beatrice was holding the boys when he walked in and

he said, "There's my boys!" and kissed them and hugged Beatrice.

"How did it go?" Beatrice was anxious.

"It's a sad case but they are safe for now. That's all I can say right down. What's my Cain and Caleb been up to today?"

"Well can you tell me which is which?" asked

Roscoe immediately he looked at the arm bracelet, "This one is Cain, so that one is Caleb!" he grinned at her.

She pointed to her boobs, "Now which one suck this one and which that one?" He said, "I did, case closed."

Unitus was walking near the courthouse when he saw her on the steps. He walked right up to her and said, "Adriana Buchanan. How are you doing? Long time no see!"

He kissed her on the cheek and grabbed the arm that was about to slap him. He had her around the waist and pulled her up to him. Her pale blue eyes were penetrating daggers into his, and she was vivid. He said, "If you squirm it will arouse me, so stand still ... I want to take a good look at you."

He inhaled her perfume, "CIARA." Her skin was flawless and her navy suit was way too big for this toned lithe body. Body that was all of five feet ten in three inch navy heels. Yes he was sizing her up.

She was almost … almost as tall as he. His six foot two frame was pure muscle and she could feel every ounce of it. Her jaw dropped as if to speak, but instead just licked her lips and stared back into his eyes of cobalt blue.

She was trembling against him and he said, "We have a mutual friend that says you have the HOTS for me. Is that true?"

"Take your hands off me before I have you arrested," she said between her clenched teeth.

He let her go and she almost fell. By the time she had straightened, he was gone.

Unitus was not interested, she had no balls! He liked a woman with spirit. She was a looker. He gave her that.

He may sit in one of her court cases to see how her mind worked. He needed to get a shave and a haircut and pump some iron. He had a new undercover job in Dallas and he had to look the part.

A Business Man … Short hair, it would be. Clean shaven, it would be...... New Armani suits, silk ties, and Wing-tipped shoes. ALL crap as far as he was concerned.

He had a four year degree from Harvard so "crap" should not be in his vocabulary. It was residual from his last job.

"Switch gears old boy. Strike that! Thirty-two was not old." He must get a conservative swimsuit, too. The Speedo was a dead giveaway.

Most women did not think a body builder had … a brain.

Most lawyers did not have ... a body. Touche!

He could feel what he could not see … she had a body. He would love to reassess her in a string bikini.

Damn Jana was right … I am already obsessing over her and I have no frigging idea why? Strike .... frigging.

"I usually don't have a problem switching from one character to another. This woman could be dangerous to my health … or is it I just need to get laid."

He was talking to himself that was another bad sign. He found himself researching her profile. Daughter of billionaire Marcus Buchanan. Hmm ... Why would she be working as a DA? She must have some morals. "I have none," he laughed. "So my buddy, Bruce says."

Jana said, "Opposites attract, look at me and Bruce!"

Bruce said, "That is a powder keg of a woman that I am married to, pure TNT!" talking about Jana.

I told him, "Yeah, ... I and about 400 inmates heard you screaming her name. I want one JUST like her!"

"Wonder if Lady Long Legs that's her code name I am told, Can make me scream like that?" Hmm …

Jana picked this one out for me, and she knows me well.

She has for many years. I'll give it a shot! He went online and found the dockets for tomorrow. She had a case at 2:30PM … PERFECT!

He got a manicure- pedicure since in the prison system, they had no such amenities … LOL

CHAPTER THREE

At 2:30, he was sitting in the second row. He had paid a man $100 to take his seat.

She came strutting in with an armful of papers. Her client was a Japanese man. She spoke to him in fluent Japanese.

"Your Honor, may I approach the bench?"

She had on a charcoal gray pin-striped business suit today that fitted her like a glove… "a latex glove"... strike that!That was his wish list. A white clip held her mossy brunette hair up in one swoop. Damn! He wanted to squeeze it and let it fall. She had white ankle strapped three inch heels on those nice small ankles for a tall woman.

White pearl studded earrings in those tiny little ears that was attached to that gorgeous neck about then, she turned. Her pale blue eyes locked with his cobalt blues, and he saw her mouth open wide … and she swallowed what she was going to say.

There he sat in a cobalt blue double- breasted suit. His hair was short and cut to accentuate his cheek bones and clean shaven like she liked a man's face to be.

She swayed her hips a little more than he remembered as she walked back to the table ... "Continuance granted."

Her client was thanking her and they were gone.

He decided not to get up but sit out the next case which was boring. He just had to settle his libido. With it in check, he left the courthouse. He went straight to the gym and worked out till nothing on him would flex. He showered and put on his Levis and his Henley T-shirt of cobalt blue and his Salvatore "Parigi" snakeskin shoes. He did love comfortable shoes.

He had hung his suit in his locker and splashed his Armani cologne on before locking the locker. He had two locks on it, his and the club's.

Out he went to find something to eat ... as he rounded the corner. He saw her come out of the women's locker room door. This has to be unreal ... she must have found out where he was ... no his ego was out of control.

There she stood as if frozen. She had on a Vintage Versace Crop top in pale blue to match her eyes. Her midriff showed her six-pack tapering to a flat stomach. No low rider jean could hide it. She had on Fit-Flops on her long narrow feet She loved comfortable shoes, too.

He focused on her shoes to regroup his thoughts.

"So we hang out at the same places ... that's a shocker," he finally managed to say.

"You hang out at courthouses?" she pursued her lips and applied clear lip gloss.

"No. I went specifically to see you ... present a case, ...but I got cheated," and he grinned just to see, if she would smile. Her hair was halfway down her back and she flipped it.

Flipped it over one shoulder and it was cascading down in layers... now she had him drooling. Any other time, he would have turned and walked away.

I saw you working out and I was impressed," she was walking closer.

"I thought you might hurt something," and then she took her fingers and wiggled them so they touched him, ... one, two, three... across his broad back.

"Okay if we are playing touchy feely … It's my turn."

He walked closer and took one finger … his index finger and touched one ab...then two ...and the third right below her navel! She sucked in her stomach and inhaled a deep breath. She was having a hard time breathing and she saw he was ... when he touched her ABS. Her nipples hardened and strained against her top that confirmed it. She had no bra on and with those jeans, there was no room for undies. By then, he was matching her breathing pattern.

He was hardening, too! She could not keep her eyes off it as it grew.

"See what you have done to me?" he said.

Her nipples were really hard and protruding out from under her top. He saw her bare breasts heaving.

"See what you have done to me?"she said.

"What do you want to do about it?" he asked.

"What do you want to do about it?" she asked.

"I don't want to get arrested," he said.

"I'm beyond that!" she said.

She was saying, let's do it! He had to be sure … "I don't want you in the middle of the street ... but I will if that is what you want. I'd rather have you in my bed all night long!"

"I had rather you take me here ... there … and everywhere. Do I make myself clear?"

"Perfectly!"

He picked her up and she fought him … "Put me down!" Then she jumped and straddled him, wrapping her long legs around his waist. She threw he head backwards and said, "That's more like it!"

He did not know whether he could get to the car, before he gave her what she was begging for, but he was going to damn sure try.

"God Almighty be still! You are killing me!" He got her in the car and lowered the seat. She had got her fit-flops off and her jeans. He unzipped and drove it into her like a jackhammer.

"Don't you dare stop! I am almost there!" she said and it was almost simultaneous erupting and the rippling forever … still locked together.

She said, "Me on top PLEASE! Here it comes again! He flipped her over. She rode him until he was gritting his teeth to stay hard. He was not going to let her have the upper hand.

There she lay, limp on him.

She was slowing down and it was feeling so damn good and her breast was in his mouth and he sucked it. Her vagina tightened and relaxed. He sucked it and it tightened around him. He was like a lion in the jungle he roared, and went on it again. She was squealing, "OH baby!"

Then she slumped forward. She was rubbing his nipples through his Henley. He hadn't even took his shirt off … nor had she. She lay on him … feeling of his body as if to remember every aspect of him. He decided to do the same.

"What do you say we go back in the gym and get a shower or go to my place and eat each other from head to toe."

"Your place is it .. a building... do I have to walk through?"

"No Adriana I have a ranch house rented over on White Rock Lake. You can just stay as you are and I will carry you in … without a peeping tom noticing."

"I am so hard for you already … doesn't make sense."

"Sounds good! I'll just lay my head in your lap while you drive."

He was driving and she was kissing and he was about to lose his mind. He stopped on the side of the road and did her good.

She just grinned and said, "Is that all you got? It was sooo good, I want more."

"Behave until we get home and you can have all you want!"

He stood up and she wrapped her long legs around her, and kissed his neck as he walked.

He put the key in the door and they fell onto the soft cool leather couch and he climbed between her legs.

Bruce and Jana said you were perfect for me. "You are so perfect. You fit so DAMN perfect. OH my goodness you can't be doing that again!"

"Shut up and please me! Women want it just as bad as men … only I say … what I want … Now tell me what you want?"

He simply said, "YOU."

She said, "You got me."

He said, "For how long?"

"Till I have to be in court tomorrow at 2:00PM. Can you handle that?"

"I will handle anything you will give me. I am afraid you are going to be the death of me, but I don't care. You have me ... Hook Line and Sinker!"

"You are talking crazy. You are just saying what you think I want to hear. I am no lame bimbo."

"Let's go Bimbo," and he took her shirt off and threw her over his shoulder after he had stripped his own clothes off, then walked them to the shower."

"Caveman … no one has ever picked me up. I am too tall and mean. I kick, and bite … if anyone comes near me." He was soaping her up in the shower and she was talking a mile a minute … "I don't want you to think I jump in the bed with just every Tom, Dick, and Harry … I was just fascinated by you … I didn't want to lose you."

"You will never lose me. Marry me? ADRIANA! Are you okay?" She had fainted.

"Was that a yes?" he laid her on the bed, her eyes fluttered.

"Are you ready to be my wife? When you know you know. YOU and I are not dummies. I know and I want to hear you say it ..."

"Yes, I will think about it!" she quipped. He grabbed her and sat her own him like she liked it. She said "Yes!" He said,"Yes!" and they did this until they climaxed.

"You would have thought we were a couple of teenagers last night. It could have been splashed all over today's paper. Prosecutor arrested for indecent exposure and all she could do was waving like Miss America to the adoring crowd."

"Yes I do feel like a teenager with you … you would not have had me then … I was scared of women!" he was moaning because she was licking his lips as he spoke." A ring will be on that finger before tomorrow and you can count on that prosecutor." "Sit Still."

"Say it! We … are going … to the Justice of the Peace before five today!" He was withholding what she wanted!.

She was writhing and he was strong enough to stand her against the wall.

"Say it again and again and again!" He didn't hear what she said. He was in the throes of passion and gnawing on her shoulder and filling her for the sixth time. "Yes!" and she melted into him. They were one.

They were standing in business attire standing in the back room of the Judge's chambers.

"You know I have OK 'd a marriage license to be rushed to me and I will save you from the crowd. By marrying you in here, you two can go out the back. I'll have my car brought around. That is this Judge's wedding present to you, Adriana."

He was frowning with his glasses falling onto the bridge of his nose. The Judge said, "You will have to be my buffer. Your father will be coming after my head!"

She said in her most diplomatic voice, "I have your request. I have it filed in my top desk drawer, your honor. Father will reward you greatly when he is holding our first child," she smiled at Unitus who had gone pale.

Out the back door and into the black limo that sped off to the airport. She had her colleague Brian Graham to take her cases for a week. Unitus had his business deal deferred to another agent.

They were having a mile high adventure in whomever's plane. She said, "IT just gets better and better. Where are we going?"

"To a little town in North Carolina called Hendersonville, You will recognize the people who are picking us up at the Charlotte Airport," he grinned.

"They have twenty bedrooms ..." her eyes got big.

"I did not want to see a soul I knew while on our honeymoon. I brought no clothes!" Her mouth was going ninety miles an hour. He reached and kissed her and kept it shut for a good while. The pilot hit a few unnecessary bumps and rolls... just to let Unitus know he could hear Unitus screaming "Adriana!"

Barry Turner was one of Unitus's colleagues. He had flown him to many dangerous missions.

"Congrats dude!" they chest bumped.

"Can I kiss the bride?" Barry asked.

"Get away from her or your life is gone!" Unitus was grinding his teeth and pointing in Barry's face. Adriana was terrified and they began laughing and he patted Barry on the back.

"Sure you can, if she will let you! Warning, she is possessed

She bites!" Unitus was looking at the grin that was forming on Adriana's lips.

She said to him, "And don't you ever forget it!" Her eyes were sparkling.

She barely let Barry hug her. She never took her eyes off Unitus … who was pacing.

"Barry I think we are going back on the plane. My wife says she forgot something!" Staring at Adriana. She was grabbing his, and he caught her hand. She licked her lips and walked back into the plane.

Barry said, "I want one like that!" he was nodding his head.

"We need to catch our ride. Where do you want to live?"

"Unitus everything does not have to be voted on, decided, or argued about in seven days... We have better things to do my burly muscular hubby!" and she walked into the ladies room at the airport.

There she took out of her outfit from her oversized shoulder bag. Putting on her VETEMENTS sweats made in Paris of hunter green and donning her bisque Helmut Lang Shearling coat. She brushed her teeth applied a small amount foundation and lined her eyes with hunter green eyeliner. She pulled her hair up in a high ponytail.

Fifteen minutes later, she walked out.

The payoff was seeing Unitus's eyes, then he spoke.

"I thought you had fallen in," he said. She gave him the look ... the I cannot believe you said that look.

"Holy! I should ... I meant to say... You look fabulous!" He saw the hunter green eyeliner that meant she have taken extra care to look her best for him! "Forgive me angel?"

"I can't believe you said that either!" and she walked on.

Bruce and Jana were waiting at the baggage claims. Unitus was waiting for Adriana who was finally smiling.

Hugging Jana and high-fiving Bruce, he was her client. She had a rule about that.

Unitus hugged Bruce and patted Jana on the top of her head before hugging her.

"These two check my height to see... if I have grown any since the last time. Jana explained Unitus's gesture.

"Isn't that disrespectful?" Adriana stood with arms crossed then trying to lower herself so she could hear Jana better.

The airport was crowded and everyone was talking and laughing … as were Bruce and Unitus … but his eyes never left Adriana and her eyes never left his.

"It is so good of you to invite us!"

"Unitus is always invited anywhere we are ... Japan, Dallas, N Carolina. He is like family. Only he keeps saving my husband's life. I love him for that. Beware if Unitus needs him ... Bruce will be there for him, and I cannot him not to."

"OMG I just got married to a guy that may get killed

any day. I love him beyond my imagination and I just got mad at him over nothing!"

"It happens ... but never go to bed angry. Fuss and fight all day, but before bedtime make up," Jana said.

"Unitus said you picked me out for him. Why?"

"You could tame him. No woman has ever come close, Adriana," and she smiled.

Adriana smiled at Unitus and he turned around to see, if someone was behind him. Bruce was killing himself laughing at Unitus.

"She's got you turning around in circles, not in this lifetime would I have believed it." Bruce said.

"Oh," smiling back at Adriana."Shut your mouth Bruce before I kill you!" Bruce could not help it, he was laughing so hard.

Unitus said, "If you can't then I am going elsewhere to stay," smiling at the women. "Seriously stop!"

Bruce patted Unitus, "I know how it feels I have been there. You gave me grief over".... smiling at the women... "my goo goo eyes at Jana. "You do understand now?"

"Crystal clear," he waved the girls over. Kissing his beautiful bride on the cheek for fear what might happen, if he kissed her on the lips. She was not having it ... she put both arms around his neck.

He said softly, "Let me tell you something, darling that man over there will never let me live it down. If I have to walk to that door with this erection.... Do you feel it? Let me have your coat to put across my arm ... I will give you all this gladly anywhere in the world … but not here. I promise!"

"I will not stay here and cannot jump your bones when … I want some!"

"You are making it grow ... stop that talk. It turns me on. Help me wifey!"

Jana said, "You have teased him enough, he won't stay. Now apologize, you may need her in less than six months."

He kissed her, "You are right, my Jana!"

"Truce . Sorry Unitus … Forgive!" He couldn't shake, it would move the coat. So Adriana shook his hand, "We accept your apology," and she dragged him to the white limo.

Bruce had told Roscoe he was picking him up, "Take the limo, "Unitus is a little bit too big for Beatrice's Miata and I have to have my Silverado for work. Grandma won't be home till Friday, so go on and enjoy!"

Bruce had phoned James and he was there to pick them up.

Adriana and Jana shopped at a mall and purchased some things for Adriana. She never shopped. Jana was showing her the fun of it. She was teaching this sophisticated woman a trick or two about lingerie, "I just don't wear any."

Jana's eyes bugged out, "But that is what men like!"

Adriana shook her head, "Not mine," she shook her head again. "More than six times a day and I am dead tired. Of course, I have only known him for four days. He has made me the happiest I have ever been."

Jana said, "Explain?"

"Yes the sex is great! I mean great!" She sat on a mall bench. "I have never had a man want me for me. No ulterior motive. Usually it has been to get to my daddy or get a friend out of jail, etc. The list goes on and on. He is intellectually stimulating, good looking, fits me like a glove ..."

"Stop I get the picture," and they both laughed. "You need no lingerie now, but think about it in the future."

James was loading all the packages in the trunk and the girls were getting in. When Adriana said to Unitus, "I bet you thought I fell in," she was rubbing his thigh.

Jana asked, "Fell in where?"

Unitus was so glad it was getting dark, "Inside joke." He was holding both of Adriana's hands and kissing her fingertips.

Bruce said, "Anyone hungry?"

Unitus said, "Starving! Not for food!" looking into his wife's eyes who was equally as eager from the way she was twisting in her new jeans. "These aren't as comfortable as I thought they would be ... If it is a long ride, I think I will go and change!"

"I think I will go and help her," Unitus said. They went down to the jacuzzi area and pulled the curtain, and turned the music up. Unitus was trying to get his boots off.

"Leave them on ... and lay back." Her stretch jeans were off in a flash. He said, "You sure do like to be in charge." He gasped as she straddled him," and he said "I love it!" They took five turns on who was in charge and they fell asleep in the jacuzzi.

Bruce and Jana went in and left the lovebirds in the car, as did James.

Bruce told Jana, "They will eventually wake up and come in or not!"

Unitus was cooking bacon and six eggs. "I have to eat to keep my strength up," winking at her. Adriana was eating oatmeal. They were so different, but yet alike.

Bruce and Jana had left a NOTE that they were going to the hospital to see the babies. There are two Black Russian terriers in the barn. They will not bother you unless you hold her down and she screams. I have to put a gag in Jana's mouth! LOL"

Unitus said, "I am so glad you are not a screamer."

"Me, too … But you are! Don't worry sweetheart I will gag you, I promise!" she winked at her husband.

Roscoe had hired a nurse to stay with Beatrice and the boys when he was not home. Her name was Angie and she had been oriented to the house by Guy and him. WE want you to know both the houses encase one house need you worse. If you have a friend that is as equally qualified, please leave her name and phone number by the phone with second nurse written under the name. Angie wrote Laurie and her number.

It was a cacophony getting the boys home and into the nursery. He was catering to Beatrice who was not able to get up the steps. Let alone, be left alone with the babies. Now he wished he had agreed to the elevator Guy wanted to install.

He told him, "You have three floors I only have two. We won't need it! Wrong! Boy, do we need it!"

They finally got everyone feed. The nurse and Beatrice sat and wrote a schedule for them to follow and attached it to the refrigerator door.

Roscoe said, "Where is the refrigerator? Downstairs."

"Tomorrow honey, I will get a small fridge delivered to the boys room."

She said, "Thank you, darling. I will pump these boobies and store milk in it. So you and I can feed them at the same time. This whipping them out in public is not for me. So when we go out for the day, we can just grab some bottles from our whittle bitty fridge!" she was grinning.

"I am so glad you are home," he said, kissing her.

She said, "Me, too!"

In the house across the lake was Kyleigh and Guy. The baby was feeding and Guy was watching. All he had to do was go get the baby and hand him to Kyleigh. No bottles, no formula, not even a little refrigerator on the second floor.

He was not going to work for a little bit. Just spend this time with Kyleigh and Madison. The doctor told him to watch for postpartum depression. It had scared him and he had not told anyone, he would tell GM when she got home.

Trevor and Madeline were on their way home. The dogs were in their crates and settled. The plane would arrive in Charlotte around 3:00PM and James would pick them up. They knew Bruce and Jana, Unitus and Adriana were at the house.

Guy got his dog and Roscoe had got his dog. Their dogs would have no problems going into their stable homes because they were the same as the Dallas stables at Southfork.

Only one problem, their was a visitor in the stable. Trevor got his rifle and Bruce got his pistol, and Unitus was to protect the women.

The dogs ran and ran until, they cornered it. It was Big Black Bear eating the dogs' food.

Trevor said, "Let him have it. I'll buy them some more. Take the dogs in Bruce and we'll go over to Guy's and get some dog food for them in a few."

The women were loving on the dogs and Unitus had brought in the dog crates.

"It is so good to see you Adriana. Did your father tell you the news?" Madeline said.

"What news?" Adriana asked.

"He bought Smith Oil from us on Monday!"

She looked shocked. She looked at Unitus. He didn't know.

When Bruce returned, Adriana walked to him and asked, "Why didn't you of all people tell me MY father bought your mother's company. So Unitus is like a brother. YOU all are in on this deal. Call me a cab!"

Jana ran to her, "You are wrong, so wrong!"

Jana said, "Tell her Unitus! Tell her!"

"She will not believe a word I say. I saw the look she gave me. She is too much like me. I would probably think the same thing. It will take time. I think I will walk through the woods and punch me a bear."

There on her desk was a letter. She had looked at it all day. She could not open it until she was through with her cases for the day.

Then at her apartment, she opened the envelope.

SHE READ THE FOLLOWING!

Anywhere in the world I could have taken you for our honeymoon, but I wanted you to meet my family....My mother and father are dead. I have no brothers or sisters. That's why I chose the job that I do. No ties. No one to answer to but myself. Until I met you...
I thought you were different. I could see the same hollowness in your eyes. I thought you were my equal and then you slaughtered my new found family and ripped my heart out of my chest.. I will not come to you because I have not done anything wrong, nothing to apologize for ... I still love you my wife! I have a one year mission which you will not be able to break this code. Just know I love you till death do us part! Unitus

To be continued